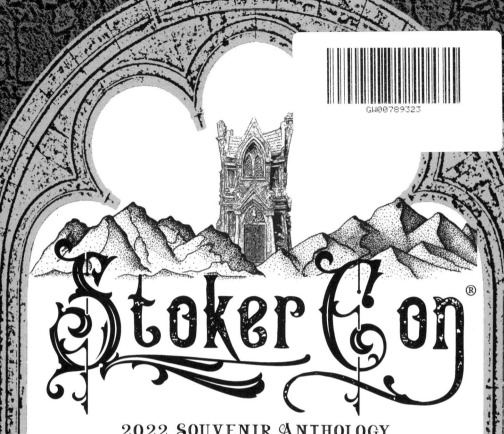

StokerCon®

2022 Souvenir Anthology

The Denver Resurrected Edition

EDITED BY

Cynthia Pelayo

STOKERCON® 2022 SOUVENIR ANTHOLOGY
THE DENVER RESURRECTED EDITION

Print ISBN: 978-1-957918-00-6
First Edition: May 2022

"Delivery" previously appeared in *Stories For the Next Pandemic,* © 2020 by Brian Keene;
"Barefoot and Midnight" previously appeared in *Apex* Magazine, © 2021 by Sheree Renée Thomas;
"Years of Decay" previously appeared in *The Healing Monsters Vol. 1,* © 2016 by John Edward Lawson;

Edited by Cynthia Pelayo
Technical Edits by Gerardo Pelayo
Copyedits by Karmen Wells | Shelf-Made Creative
Beta read by Ross Jeffery
Cover art by Kealan Patrick Burke | Elderlemon Design
Interior layout and design by Todd Keisling | Dullington Design Co.
Art direction by Cynthia Pelayo & Todd Keisling

Illustrations by Todd Keisling, Ryan Mills, & Lenka Šimečkova

Published by Burial Day Books, LLC.
Chicago, Illinois
www.BurialDay.com

TABLE OF CONTENTS

IN MEMORIAM
    LISA MANNETTI.. 9
    JOE MCKINNEY.. 15
    WILLIAM F. NOLAN... 19
    ANNE RICE... 21
    PETER ADAM SALOMON... 27
    DAVE THOMAS.. 31

WELCOME HOME: A LETTER FROM THE EDITOR
    BY CYNTHIA PELAYO... 35

HWA ANTI-HARASSMENT POLICY... 39

OMICRON, DELTA, AND CONVENTIONS...OH MY!
    BY JAMES CHAMBERS & BRIAN W. MATTHEWS 47

THE NEW FACES OF THE HWA
    BY JOHN PALISANO.. 49

THE BRAM STOKER AWARDS®
    EMCEE: KEVIN J. WETMORE, JR. 53
    KEYNOTE SPEAKER: LINDA D. ADDISON............................ 55

STOKERCON® 2022 GUESTS OF HONOR
    ERNEST DICKERSON... 59
    GEMMA FILES 75
    BRIAN KEENE 89

TABLE OF CONTENTS

John Edward Lawson 115

Jennifer McMahon 139

Sheree Renée Thomas 151

The 2021 Bram Stoker Awards® Final Ballot 169

The HWA Lifetime Achievement Award 175

Jo Fletcher 177

Nancy Holder 181

Koji Suzuki 185

Specialty Press Award 187

Mentor of the Year Award 191

The Silver Hammer Award 195

The Richard Laymon President's Award 199

Ann Radcliffe Academic Conference: Five Years of Fear and Loathing
by Michele Brittany & Nicholas Diak 203

StokerCon® Librarians' Day 2022
by Konrad Stump 205

Alone in the Dark: The Final Frame Film Festival
by Jonathan Lees 209

Horror University: At the Heart of StokerCon and the HWA's Mission
by James Chambers 211

HWA Poetry Showcase: The Point of Poetry
by Angela Yuriko-Smith 215

Pitch Sessions
by Rena Mason & Brian W. Matthews 219

A Literary History of Denver
by Maria Abrams 221

A Ghostly Line: Balancing Being a Writer with Being a Parent
by Christa Carmen 225

The Village Through the Side of the Horror House
Rhonda Jackson Garcia 231

If You Give a Bookstore A Horror Section
by Sadie Hartmann 237

Finding Hope in Horror
by Rayne King 243

A Little Less Haunted Than Before
by Eric LaRocca 247

TABLE OF CONTENTS

Why Horror Is My Home
    by Janine Pipe.. 251
Going Within
    by Mary Rajotte.. 257
Writing During Difficult Times
    by Tim Waggoner.. 261
Afterword
    by Meghan Arcuri 265
About the Horror Writers Association 269
About the Bram Stoker Awards® 271
About the Editor
    Cynthia Pelayo 275
About the Technical Editor
    Gerardo Pelayo 277
About the Copyeditor
    Karmen Wells 279
About the Cover Artist
    Kealan Patrick Burke... 281
About the Book Designer
    Todd Keisling 283
About the Illustrators
    Ryan Mills 285
    Lenka Šimečkova.. 285
About the Beta Reader
    Ross Jeffery 287
The Bram Stoker Awards® committee for 2021 289
Acknowledgments... 291
Souvenir Book Sponsorships 295

Selected Artwork
    Todd Keisling 46, 116, 140, 229, 273
    Ryan Mills 6, 56, 102, 126, 137, 214, 235, 268
    Lenka Šimečkova..38, 76, 179, 241

REMEMBERING LISA MANNETTI
by Sèphera Girón

A ward-winning horror author Lisa Mannetti left us in the summer of 2021, during a world-wide pandemic. She didn't die from COVID-19 or any of its related illnesses. She died after a long battle with cancer.

Lisa was a well-loved member of the horror community for the past couple of decades. She was friendly and had no problem infiltrating any conversation. She often made the recipients of her attention feel special and important. Stories of her generosity have circulated since her untimely death. There are countless anecdotes of Lisa helping people whether it was paying for a night at the Lizzie Borden Bed and Breakfast, helping people with airfare to attend a convention, or donating her time and energy to mentor writers and even connecting them with publishers.

I'd seen Lisa around over the years at conventions. However, I distinctly remember the first time I talked to her. It was at one of the HWA NYC weekends and her mother had just died. She was walking with a cane, and I believe that was the only time I ever saw her with a cane. She had pulled her knee before the con. She kept going out on the balcony to smoke, of course. She might have even been smoking inside at the table as well, that's how long ago it was. Everyone was smoking everywhere in those days. I'm not sure how our conversation began, I seem to recall she tripped when she was walking with her cane, and I went over to help her. I ended up sitting with her at some point and she told me how her mom had just died. One conversation led into another, as it always did with Lisa.

The next time we really interacted was the year my car broke down on the way to Necon. I was trapped in Rhode Island waiting for car repairs. Lisa said a bunch of campers were staying over at the Lizzie Borden House that night and I should join them. I'd heard her talk before at Necon parties about how the Lizzie Borden House was haunted. Over the years, before that point, she had arranged for day tours for Necon campers, but I never went. I didn't believe in haunted houses. But that fatal day I was trapped in Rhode Island, so I figured, why not go hang out with other horror authors in a murder house. I believe there were thirteen of us that year. Only recently did I realize that was the first time she rented out the whole house for the night. We all chipped in, of course. A lot of freaky stuff happened that first night. At one point, Lisa and I were so scared, we stood on the porch in a violent sudden summer storm, chain-smoking and trying to book a hotel somewhere else while lightning and thunder crashed around us. After that night, I believed in haunted houses.

That trip began a nearly annual tradition of renting out the Lizzie Borden house whenever Lisa went to Necon (which was always held the third week of July). The Lizzie Borden tradition was a lot of fun and that was when I really had a chance to hang out with Lisa. We always would get Lizzie a birthday cake as the retreat was around Lizzie's birthday and sometimes actually on her birthday. Lisa would always want us to light the candles and sing to Lizzie and we'd all always look around nervously while singing to see if we'd activated any spirits.

The group always went for a fancy dinner at a local restaurant in Fall River while we waited for the day tours of the house to end, and our rooms readied. After a nice dinner, we'd return to the house which would always feel a bit spookier as the sun set. We'd hire a Borden tour guide to regale new people with historical tales of the house. A couple of times, we hired local mediums for seances, but the mediums were always fake. Lisa and I would run our own seances in the living room, by the couch where Andrew Borden had his head axed in. Twice, Lisa and I used the house Ouija board, but we were freaked out by it. Lisa was a great tarot card reader and we'd both conduct readings for whoever joined us on our haunted murder house adventures. There are way too many tales of terror to reveal here.

Lisa had a special affinity with Lizzie and always slept in her room for the three hours we'd try to sleep. Lisa would say that she was terrified of sleep paralysis in that room, that she'd be frozen and hear things all around as if Lizzie herself was holding her prisoner. Yet, she would sleep there. Much like how I always slept in Andrew Borden's room even though I was terrified of him.

Corrine de Winter would bring her equipment for her podcast, and we'd do live mediumship readings and interviews on the air with whoever was at the house that time. Lisa was always ready to confirm "Lizzie did it" on the air.

Although my fondest memories of Lisa are from being terrorized at the Lizzie Borden house, we had fun at other places as well such as after the Stokers one year in Burbank. We had a tour of the Forever Hollywood graveyard with a few other horror writers and enjoyed hearing Hal Bodner tell us stories about the various celebrities. We also had a blast at the very first StokerCon® in Las Vegas a few years later.

Lisa had planned for me and her to attend StokerCon® in England in 2020. She wanted us to go a week early, rent a car and tour the moors as she'd always wanted to see the moors. She wanted a companion to go with her as it was a foreign country, to help with the driving, and, personally, I think because she was often stricken with various illnesses at the most inopportune times. However, she realized she had to stay home to care for her ill husband but was still trying to finagle a way for us to attend even without making it a two-week adventure. Then the pandemic hit and StokerCon® was cancelled anyway.

A few months later, Lisa complained of being tired. It reminded me of that ominous line from *Evita*, "she looked tired" and I had a bad feeling about it all. A couple of months later, she was in the hospital. Little did any of us know that this was her last dance. One of the last real conversations I had with her was in September 2020 when she said she had so many wires coming out of her that she looked like Robbie the Robot. She was moved back home. Then no one could get through on her phone for months. In the spring of 2021, she had a brief rejuvenation that I heard about through friends. She was growing hair and her phone was plugged in. I only called her a couple of times because it hurt her to speak, and she couldn't say much. Yet she continued to laugh and make plans for the future in our thirty second phone call. I was so hopeful her spunky spirit was going to beat this...whatever it was. She never told me she had cancer...

The last time I saw her was at Necon in 2019. She had kindly treated me that year as my financial situation was a disaster, and we were roommates again. We all thought she escaped death that year as she was T-boned turning left into the road that led to the convention center. Not long after she returned home, her house caught on fire, and again, we breathed with relief that she had escaped death once more. But the third time was not the charm for Lisa. She couldn't escape cancer.

Lisa was a talented award-winning author.

Many years ago, she was working on a book about Mount Everest and the ghosts of dead hikers. I was helping her with edits as she wrote various chapters and I really thought it was a cool book. I don't think she ever finished it, although parts of it made it into a short story. A recent book she was working on was about the radium girls. I see that radium girls is currently a popular topic even though she first was dreaming about it years ago. She had a knack for knowing what people wanted to read.

She won Stokers for her novel, *The Gentling Box* and the short story, "Apocalypse Then."

She was also nominated for:

- "ArbeitMacht Frei" (*Gutted: Beautiful Horror Stories*, Crystal Lake Publishing), Short Fiction, 2016
- *The Box Jumper* (Smart Rhino Publications), Long Fiction, 2015
- "The Hunger Artist" (*Zippered Flesh 2*, Smart Rhino Publications), Short Fiction, 2013
- *Dissolution*, Long Fiction, 2010
- "1925: A Fall River Halloween," Short Fiction, 2010

Her story, "Everybody Wins" was made into the short film "Bye Bye Sally" and her novella, *Dissolution*, is in the works to be a feature-length film both directed by Paul Leyden. Her short stories include "Esmeralda's Stocking" in *Never Fear: Christmas Terrors*; "Resurgam" in *Zombies: More Recent*

Dead edited by Paula Guran, and "Almost Everybody Wins," in *Insidious Assassins*. Her work, including The *Gentling Box*, and "1925: A Fall River Halloween" has been translated into Italian.

Her work also includes *The New Adventures of Tom Sawyer and Huck Finn*, two companion novellas in *Deathwatch*, *51 Fiendish Ways to Leave your Lover*, as well as non-fiction books, numerous articles, and short stories.

Corrine de Winter is in charge of Lisa's literary estate.

Rest in Power, Lisa. I miss our phone calls.

REMEMBERING JOE McKINNEY
by J. G. Faherty

O n July 13, 2021, we lost a very special member of our genre, Joe McKinney.

In Memoriams are always so hard to write. It's important that we honor and remember our fellow writers who have passed, but putting the words to paper, and/or reading them, not only brings back the sadness, but also somehow makes the loss more permanent, as if there is no way we can pretend the person is just taking a social media break and we'll hear from them in a few weeks.

This one is especially hard, because I considered Joe one of my friends and mentors in this business.

I first met Joe somewhere around 2010-2011, not long after I was elected as an HWA Board Trustee for the first time. Joe was already on the board, and in the beginning we only chatted via email and through social media, mostly about HWA business. Then I got to meet him in person at events, including the HWA's first Library Programming event, part of the American Library Association's Winter Convention. I was running our library program at the time, and Joe was one of the people I asked to spend the weekend there presenting on panels. He gladly obliged; one of the things I would come to know about Joe is that he was always ready and willing to help new writers and horror readers.

Over the next few years, we got to be very friendly, and although we lived on opposite sides of the country and I am terrible at making/responding to phone calls, we spoke fairly often via Facebook. At first, a lot of our conversations were me asking him questions about police procedure. A sergeant with the San Antonio Police Department, Joe was always glad to help, and he'd tell me stories of things that happened on the job and how those events influenced his writing. He had a quirky, low-key sense of humor that I appreciated, and always had a smile on his face when I'd see him at conventions. In 2011, I was lucky enough to share a table of contents with him for *Best New Zombie Tales, Vol. 3*. I remember congratulating each other on that one not long after we'd met for the first time in person.

As we got to know each other, we discovered we both had a love of cooking, and we'd often share recipes or just talk about meals we'd enjoyed. I know Joe had many other friends in the industry, and he was always happy to beta read someone's story, help them with a submission, work on story plots, and even recommend magazines or anthologies that were opening up for submissions. He loved talking writing and helping writers. That is how I'll remember him best. But it's not all he was.

In addition to being an all-around good guy and friend, Joe was an excellent writer in his own right. His work in the zombie genre, including his Dead World novels, along with novels such as *Inheritance, The Savage Dead,* and *Dog Days*, cemented him as a top author in the horror world, and earned him two Bram Stoker Awards® (*Flesh Eaters, Dog Days*). But for me, his true genius was his short stories, and his collection, *The Red Empire and Other Stories*, is one of the few collections to not only give me shivers but make me envious of how fantastic the stories were. I place it right up there with my all-time favorite collections, including King's *Night Shift* and Ketchum's *Peaceable Kingdom*. Not only were the stories all top-notch material, they demonstrated a broader range of material than the novels he was known for, everything from sci-fi/horror to quiet thrillers.

Joe was unique in many other ways. As a police officer, he served as a patrol officer, homicide detective, and disaster mitigation specialist, and also helped run San Antonio's 911 Dispatch Center. He studied English Literature at Oxford University but also wrote his fiction in an 'everyman' style that wasn't the least bit pretentious. His works often included a good deal of realism, and he wasn't afraid to tackle controversial topics, such as border relations between the US and Mexico, prejudice, sexism, and police misconduct.

One of the many sad aspects of Joe's passing is that he always said he intended to really expand his writing. I wish he'd had more of a chance. In addition to zombie novels, Joe dipped his toes in other genres, including thrillers, crime/mystery, coming-of-age YA, supernatural horror, and science fiction, putting out more than twenty novels, two collections, numerous short stories, and non-fiction articles. I know he had more mysteries and thrillers he wanted to write, and his gritty, realistic science fiction, while limited mostly to short stories, was always something to look forward to.

Joe held a BA in American History from Trinity University, where he played baseball, and an MA in English Literature from the University of Texas. His hobbies included Texas history and legends (especially the old outlaws), cooking, sightseeing, and unsolved crimes and mysteries. With the HWA, Joe served as a Trustee, Secretary of the Board, and Chapter Program Coordinator. More than anything, though, he loved spending time with his wife and daughters.

In recent years, Joe stepped back from writing horror and focused more on crime novels, which he published under a pseudonym. I missed seeing him at conventions, but we continued to stay in touch through email and social media. We enjoyed some serious but always friendly discussions about politics, the world in general, and life as a writer. After some tumultuous years, he'd finally found some real peace in his life and he was sounding happier than I'd heard him in a long time.

And then, in the blink of an eye, he was gone.

His passing is a terrible loss to the horror and crime genres, and to all the people who, like me, called him a friend.

REMEMBERING WILLIAM F. NOLAN
by R.C. Matheson

I grew up with him always around the house, volcanically funny, indefatigable, dizzyingly talented. He never treated me like a kid, and we talked and laughed for another eighty years, give or take a few zillion serious truths about life and writing.

Though a titan of brilliant twists, Bill was also a professional, race-car addict. Around him, no curve had a chance.

Farewell, my dear pal.

REMEMBERING ANNE RICE

GOODNIGHT, QUEEN OF THE DAMNED, MOTHER OF THE NIGHT

by Gabrielle Faust

We clung to the hem of her long black gown as she led us from the light into the world of the undead. Forever changed, the world around us, as the creatures of the night seduced our imaginations and hearts, dousing it in their kerosene of ethereal beauty, tragedy, blood, and agony. Death became elegance, graveyards moments of poetry and reflection. Entranced and spellbound, we found ourselves tracing the streets of New Orleans at night in hopes of a glimpse of Louis or Lestat leaning amongst the shadows of the timeless French Quarter, their inhumanly pale eyes concealed behind shades.

We howled in the bayous with her wolves and danced barefoot on brick streets with her Mayfair witches. The sweet decay of the Great Mississippi, liquor, and magnolia blooms beneath a full moon, the perfume of ritual incense wafting like spirits through the heavy Spanish moss. The achingly melancholy song of an ancient violin weaving through kudzu and night jasmine vines at midnight. The glint of fangs before the kill. The echoing emptiness of loss. Forever, were we changed, not simply intellectually or emotionally, but on a much deeper cellular level and never again did we see the world as we once did as a child.

The moment we opened the pages of *Interview with the Vampire* in 1976, we all became Anne Rice's children of the night. And today we mourn our Vampire Queen, our Great Mother's passing.

Howard Allen Frances O'Brien, later known as Anne Rice, was born on October 4th, 1941, in New Orleans, Louisiana, the city that would become the focus of many of her critically acclaimed series such as *The Vampire Chronicles*. Rice spent most of her youth in the impoverished Catholic "Irish Channel" neighborhood of New Orleans where she and her family resided in a home on St. Charles Street rented by her maternal grandmother, known to the O'Brien family as "Mamma Allen." Mamma Allen, having separated from her alcoholic husband, was employed as a domestic, working tirelessly to take care of her family as Anne's own mother was slowly consumed by her own battle with alcoholism.

After Mamma Allen's passing in 1949, the O'Brien family stayed in the house until 1956 when they relocated to a former rectory and convent owned by the parish just two blocks away to be closer to the church as they sought support for Anne's mother's addiction. At the age of fifteen, after the passing of her mother, Anne and her sister were placed in the St. Joseph Academy by their father. It was a dreary, harsh institution Anne later described as "a dilapidated, awful, medieval type of place." She went on to say, "I really hated it and wanted to leave. I felt betrayed by my father." Anne's father, Howard O'Brien hastily remarried in 1957 and relocated the family to Richardson, Texas only a year later.

After graduating from Richardson High School in 1959, Anne Rice completed her freshman year at Texas Woman's University in Denton, Texas before transferring to North Texas State College for her sophomore year. Unfortunately, she was forced to drop out when she was unable to find employment and took the opportunity to move to San Francisco to live with a family friend. After convincing a former roommate from North Texas to join her, they resumed their studies at an all-male Jesuit college, the University of San Francisco, which allowed women to take courses at night. That Easter Anne returned to Texas where she "rekindled" her romance with poet and painter Stan Rice. In October of 1961 the couple was married in Denton.

A year later, in 1962, the Rices moved back to San Francisco. There, the self-proclaimed quiet, conservative Anne Rice pursued her academic studies amidst the heyday of the colorful anarchy of the Haight Ashbury hippie culture scene, typing away while the world swirled around her, eventually obtaining both a Bachelor's Degree in Political Science, as well as a Master of Arts Degree in English and Creative Writing from San Francisco State University. In 1966 Rice halted her graduate studies to become a Ph.D. student at the University of California, Berkley, but became disillusioned with the structure of Berkley's literary department, and returned to SFSU in 1970 to complete her Masters of Arts.

That same year the Rices' daughter Michele was diagnosed with leukemia at only four years of age, and by 1972 the young girl succumbed to the disease shortly before her sixth birthday. Michele's tragic death was traumatizing to the Rices', but especially poignant for Anne who later modeled her character Claudia in *Interview with the Vampire* after her lost child. Six years later, in 1978, the Rices welcomed into the world their second child, Christopher Rice.

In 1988 Anne Rice, along with her husband and son returned to her hometown of New Orleans where she purchased the historical Brevard-Rice House and settled in to craft her next novel *The Witching Hour*, followed by *Lasher* and *Taltos*, completing what she entitled *The Mayfair Witches* trilogy. The late 1980's and 90's proved to be exceedingly prolific for Rice as she continued *The Vampire Chronicles* series through ten full novels. In addition, she penned the haunting ghost story *Violin* in 1997, amongst many other stories that continued to entice and capture the imagination of millions around the globe. Since her first publication, the works of Anne Rice have sold over a hundred million copies, making her one of the best-selling authors of the modern era.

Over the course of her nearly fifty-year career, Rice successfully penned thirty-six novels. Her first novel, *Interview with the Vampire* was adapted for big screen in 1994. The film was directed by Neil Jordan and starred Tom Cruise, Brad Pitt, Kirsten Dunst, and Antonio Banderas. The third novel in *The Vampire Chronicles* series, *Queen of the Damned* was also adapted for film and released in 2000. The following year *The Feast of All Saints* was embraced by Showtime for a mini-series. And in 2011 her novel *Servant of the Bones* was acquired and transformed into a comic book mini-series. In addition, several of *The Vampire Chronicles* novels were adapted into both graphic novels and manga.

After the release of *Interview with the Vampire* Rice turned her prolific literary skills to the erotica genre publishing the novels *The Claiming of Sleeping Beauty, Beauty's Punishment,* and *Beauty's Release* under the pen name A. N. Roquelaure, followed by *Exit to Eden* (also adapted to film in 1994) and *Belinda* with the pen name Anne Rampling. Having explored the world of erotica to her satisfaction, Anne returned her sights to her beloved vampires and immersed herself deeper within their world with *The Vampire Lestat* and *Queen of the Damned.* Today *The Vampire Chronicles* series is comprised of an incredible twelve novels in and of itself.

Following the loss of her husband Stan to brain cancer, as well as two near-death experiences herself from medical complications, Rice made a return to the faith of her youth, Catholicism, in 2005, though it was not without her vocal objections to many of the Church's stances on social issues, largely LGBTQIA+ rights. Over the course of the next four years Rice turned her literary attention to her faith, penning *Christ the Lord: Out of Egypt* and *Christ the Lord: The Road to Cana,* as well as her memoir *Called Out of Darkness: A Spiritual Confession,* before once again making a "public break with organized religion" in 2010.

Throughout her career Anne Rice felt she never truly understood the vast impact her work had on the world, influencing every aspect of twentieth century culture from music and art to fashion and even cultural world perceptions. This was especially true for the Goth scene that emerged in the late seventies and instantly gravitated to the ruinous elegance, romance, and drama depicted within the pages of her novels.

In an interview for "Gothic Beauty Magazine", shortly before the release of *The Prince Lestat* in 2014, Rice remarked, "When I started writing *Interview with the Vampire,* I had no ideas really about what impact it would have," she said. "I realized it was an eccentric novel. I believed in my obsessions and my imagination, and I forged ahead, realizing it might never have a very large readership, if it was published at all."

Forever will we be thankful that she did indeed "forge ahead" — there is no amount of gratitude her fans can express to do justice to the love, loyalty, and reverence they feel. Now, and forever.

On December 11, 2021, Anne Rice was stricken ill and later that day passed from complications from a stroke at a hospital in Rancho Mirage, California at the age of eighty. She was laid to rest within her family's mausoleum in Metairie Cemetery in New Orleans.

Good night, Queen of the Damned, Mother of Night. Farewell, Vampire Queen.

REMEMBERING PETER ADAM SALOMON
by Jeff Strand

This one hurt.

It's always sad when a member of the horror writing community dies. I am, alas, at that age where friends and colleagues can die without being way older than me, and I've mourned the loss of plenty of friends that I miss seeing a couple of times a year at events like StokerCon®. Peter Adam Salomon, on the other hand, was local. I saw him on a regular basis. This wasn't one of those abstract "doesn't actually impact my day-to-day life" deaths.

I met him at the Stokers, when he was up for Superior Achievement in a Young Adult novel for *All Those Broken Angels*. He moved to Florida shortly after that, and we, along with Lynne Hansen, started the Florida chapter of the Horror Writers Association. This experience could best be summed up as "What if you started an HWA chapter, and nobody was willing to drive more than, like, ten miles for the events?" Our first meeting had five people, including the three of us, and one person who didn't actually live in Florida but was visiting family and figured he'd stop by and say hi.

Peter had a great sense of humor about this. Our only formal event was running the HWA booth at a horror convention called Asylum Tampa, an event so poorly attended that the guy at the booth next to us asked what time they actually let people into the vendor's room.

"It's been open for forty-five minutes," I told him.

"Are you shitting me?"

The advantage to tumbleweeds blowing through the room was that Peter and I got to spend *lots* of quality time together. We may not have given out many HWA brochures, but I got to talk to a fascinating guy. He claimed that the entirety of his published work contained exactly one joke (and to the best of his knowledge nobody had ever discovered it) but in person he was witty and entertaining. The Florida HWA chapter was later taken out behind the barn and shot, but Peter and I spent three days side-by-side at the HWA booth at the American Library Association conference. Though we had a lot more traffic to our booth, we also had plenty of time to talk, and it was a weekend very well spent.

When I moved to Atlanta, Peter followed. I'm not saying he followed me in a stalker manner—it could have been a coincidence, I suppose. Either way, he was fully on board when we formed the Atlanta chapter of the HWA, which was infinitely more successful than the Florida attempt. He was Vice-President, while I said you'd have to hold a chainsaw to my nether region to get me to be on the board of anything.

His volunteer work for HWA didn't stop there. I'd describe his work as "sad and poetic," and National Dark Poetry Day was his doing. He also edited the first two volumes of the *HWA Poetry Showcase*, which is now up to its eighth installment. His body of work, mostly for young adults, also includes the acclaimed *Henry Franks*, *Eight Minutes Thirty-Two Seconds*, and several installments of his *PseudoPalms* collection of fiction and poetry. (He asked me to write the foreword to the last one, and I suggested that I'm not the best choice for "sad and poetic." But he insisted, and what ensued is his own damn fault.)

His death was a shock but not a huge surprise. He had ongoing health issues, lost his job thanks to the pandemic, and had to replace it with an incredibly high-stress job that he hated—not a good combination for somebody with heart issues. The last time I saw him in person should have been at a signing we were scheduled to do together at a wine bar, but he dropped out because he wasn't feeling well. Part of the event involved having our books paired with the perfect wine accompaniment, so I made sure to get a picture of his book paired with a can of Orange Crush. He thought it was pretty funny.

So the last time I did see him was when we got together for ramen, one of my very first restaurant meals after getting vaccinated and thinking, "Finally! Things are about to get back to normal!" The ramen lunch wasn't as much fun as, say, when we went to see *Psycho: The Musical,* but still, it was a great meal with great company and as far as "last time you're going to see somebody" goes, it's a very nice memory.

Peter Adam Salomon leaves behind a fantastic body of work. He also wrote a lot more than he published—he absolutely loved creating art, loved editing anthologies, loved playing a major role in the HWA Atlanta chapter, but wasn't a huge fan of the "business" part of the writing life. My friend is gone, but there's a significant amount of his work still waiting to be read. And hopefully, someday soon it will be.

RIP, Peter.

REMEMBERING DAVE THOMAS
I SPEAK FOR THE FANS
by Brian Keene

This is not the first In Memoriam I have written for a friend in this industry. Indeed, over the last decade, I've written an even dozen. Nor is this the first In Memoriam I'll write for Dave Thomas, since his loved ones asked me to write his obituary, as well. But while the obituary focused on Dave Thomas, the man, I'd like to take this brief space to talk about Dave Thomas, the horror fiction fan who became a prominent and influential member of the professional community (which seems apt for this, the *StokerCon® Souvenir Book*).

Like many of us, Dave grew up reading horror fiction, and his passion for the genre continued into adulthood. When he graduated high school in the 1980s, Dave fled from Pennsylvania to Los Angeles, where he worked for various movie studios and video game companies. He and our friend J.F. Gonzalez used to talk breathlessly about those times —recounting not just the same concerts the two of them must have unknowingly simultaneously attended on the Sunset Strip as young men (Guns N' Roses at The Whiskey a Go Go, Poison at Gazzarri's, Motley Crue at the Troubadour,) but the book signings they also unknowingly simultaneously attended (Barker, Lansdale, King, Schow, Skipp and Spector, Laymon, Rice, Little, etc.).

Dave was intimately involved in the fan culture decades before social media elevated it to its own ecosystem. How involved? He was one of the few fans to be on hand to witness the birth of David J. Schow's seminal anthology *Silver Scream*—a veritable who's who of horror fiction's top practitioners of that time—which is why the new edition of that book is dedicated to him. Dave had an encyclopedic knowledge of the genre, and his personal library would have been enough to make scholars such as S.T. Joshi, John Pelan or S.J. Bagley salivate. He had nearly complete Arkham House and Gnome Press collections, including first editions from Lovecraft, Hodgson, Howard, Campbell and more. He had complete collections from Cemetery Dance, Delirium Books, Bloodletting Books and others. Hundreds of trade and mass market books signed by folks like Stephen King, F. Paul Wilson, Linda Addison, Yvonne Navarro, and Karl Edward Wagner. To perhaps give you an accurate idea of the size of his library—fully sixty percent of it was destroyed in a flood several years ago. The forty percent that escaped damage? Those books still take up an entire floor of the house, and I will have to spend many weekends to thoroughly catalog them for the estate.

Dave was a fan, and a collector. He never aspired to be more than that, and never thought of himself as more than that. That's why, in his later years, he was often confused by the fame and notoriety *The Horror Show with Brian Keene* brought him.

We had several fantastic co-hosts over the years—Mary SanGiovanni, Matt Wildasin, Geoff Cooper, John Urbancik, and my youngest son—but Dave was the only co-host who was there from the first episode to the last. Indeed, Dave hosted more episodes of the podcast than I did myself, and it's *my* name in the fucking title of the show.

I remember when Dave, myself, J.F. Gonzalez, and Geoff Cooper were first kicking around the idea of starting a podcast, Coop, J.F. and I said that we would be voices for the creators in the audience. Dave said, "Well, the only person I can be a voice for is the fans." Dave saw that as a small role, but for the six years we were on the air, that role blossomed into the most crucial one of all. He did indeed speak for the fans, and in doing so, he touched everyone—readers and creators alike. And as the show grew, and we went from 10 listeners to 100,000 listeners, that voice grew more important. That voice helped raise over $50,000 for charity. That voice explained issues that impacted professionals in a way that fans could understand and identify with. That voice championed the concerns of readers and consumers in a way that made professionals sit up and take notice.

In the last years of his life, Dave got a chance to see just how valued and loved he was by the writers whom he'd been reading for decades, and he was delighted by the joy and laughter and comradeship he got from his fellow fans. He saw that his singular voice made real, demonstrable, permanent differences in the field.

Horror fiction is a living ecosystem. It needs both professionals and readers to stay alive. Dave was a bridge between those two worlds. A voice that spoke for one group, and a voice which the other group paid close attention to. And while that voice has now fallen silent, and lives on only on YouTube in *The Horror Show with Brian Keene* archives, the bridge he helped build remains. And regardless of whether you're a creator or a fan, I hope you'll think of him when you're meeting in the middle of it this weekend.

WELCOME HOME
A Letter from the Editor

In 2019, at StokerCon® in Grand Rapids I was asked by poet and author Stephanie Wytovich how I would feel about participating on a panel to discuss some personal and tragic events that had interrupted my writing career. The title of that panel was 'When Your Life Becomes the Horror Story: Writing Through Personal Tragedy.' When Stephanie asked me to participate, I had just started writing again after four years of not having written much. I admit, I was fearful of discussing the reasons why I had stopped writing with a group of strangers—probably because I was trying to enter the horror writing community again and I was afraid of being stigmatized for whatever reason. But I trust Stephanie. She's a brilliant writer and poet and a compassionate person.

After reading her description of the panel, I realized that maybe some of what I would discuss on that panel may help another writer struggling. On the day of the panel, I thought, well, maybe there will be a handful of people. No, not at all. The room was nearly full. So many people were there needing and wanting to know how I and fellow authors on the panel, Brian Keene, Mary Turzillo, Stephanie Wytovich and Krystal Hammond approached our craft through times of personal crisis. All of us on the panel had lived through some catastrophic events in which we had to ask ourselves how we could possibly make it to the other side of the event that had upended our lives, while also pursuing our craft.

It was that day that I finally met Brian Keene for the first time and some of the others. I was nervous, especially because I had admired Brian Keene's career for years. So, I was scared to say why I was there for a moment, but as soon as I started talking, Brian looked over at me and told me he understood my struggles and had dealt with a similar situation in his own family. Within minutes, we were all talking and sharing very personal events, while talking passionately about wanting to create, and how we were able to do so under those circumstances.

The audience asked wonderful questions. Many of them cried. Many of them shared their own life experiences and struggles with getting words on the page after what life had just thrown at them. There were a lot of conversations after the panel too, and we met fellow writers who thanked us for being so open. Much of what we heard over and over again is that they felt relief in knowing there were other writers who were experiencing what they experienced—a life with challenges, but deadlines and dreams of writing spread before them.

I had attended StokerCons in the past, but I usually stood back as a silent observer, too afraid to introduce myself, and too afraid to talk to others about writing. Of course, I was scared of publishing rejection, but I was also afraid to be rejected by them, these creators I wished I could be like one day. But, it was that day in 2019, on that panel, when I finally felt like I found my people, like I found my home.

That's what the horror writing community has meant for me these past few years. It's been a place of hope and a place of comfort. It's been a place of creative exchanges, and sometimes some laughs and tears.

We all have been experiencing a personal tragedy in many ways, collectively as we have seen COVID impact our lives. I have seen friends in the horror writing community lose jobs, become ill, lose family members, get engaged, get married, have babies, and all the while writing, publishing, signing lucrative book and movie deals. They are pushing through with their dreams during this challenging time. Some of us, however, have gone a little quiet, to process life's changes, focusing on reading or drafting ideas and that is completely wonderful as well.

What I have also seen consistently is an immense amount of support during this time. We cheer each other's successes. We tell each other to keep going after rejection. We encourage each other to get the words on the page and to shut out the distractions of the world. We tell one another to submit that story, even when we hesitate if we should ourselves. And when we land an agent, get a story accepted, sell a book, or win an award, no one will applaud louder than your fellow horror writers. The Horror Writers Association, the horror writing community, feels like home, and I wanted to reflect that in this year's StokerCon® souvenir book.

I wanted to then in turn make the creation of this souvenir book a community project. We have multiple people throughout the horror community that have contributed their time, their words, and their artwork. I wanted to show you what we can do when we come together. Thank you to every single person who has contributed writing, artwork, formatting, editing, illustrations, and more for this book. I thank you so much.

And thank you for joining us in-person once again, and to those joining us virtually. Welcome home.

CYNTHIA PELAYO
Burial Day Books

HWA ANTI-HARASSMENT POLICY

WHAT ARE THE AIMS OF THIS ANTI-HARASSMENT POLICY?
- To help all attendees and staff feel welcome, valued, and as safe as possible.
- To define and discourage harassing, abusive behavior.
- To make it as safe and simple as possible for people to report harassment, if necessary.
- To clearly establish for staff and attendees how reports of harassment will be handled.
- To set fair consequences for such behavior.

WHY DOES STOKERCON® NEED AN ANTI-HARASSMENT POLICY?

We've implemented an anti-harassment policy in response to widespread reports of harassment at conventions and in order to meet our goal of providing a safe and comfortable convention experience for everyone.

StokerCon® is dedicated to providing a safe and comfortable convention experience for everyone, regardless of gender, sexuality, ability, physical appearance, body size, actual or perceived race, national origin, family or marital status, socio-economic class or religion. In order to offer a welcoming and safe space for everyone, we require participants to be respectful of all others and their space, be it physical or social.

WHAT IS HARASSMENT?

Harassment includes:

Offensive verbal comments about gender, sexuality, impairment, physical appearance, body size, race or religion, racist behavior, including: attendees being expected to be an authority on corresponding characters in various genre and media settings; and/or being talked down to or assumed to be less knowledgeable about topics being discussed because of ethnic origin showing sexual images in public spaces.

Discussion or images related to sex, pornography, discriminatory language or similar is permitted if it meets all of the following criteria: organizers have specifically granted permission in writing; it is necessary to the topic of discussion and no alternative exists; it is presented in a respectful manner, especially towards women and LGBTQIA people; and attendees are warned in advance in the program and respectfully given ample warning and opportunity to leave beforehand. This exception does not allow use of gratuitous sexual images as attention-getting devices (such as clothing or costumes in the dealers' room) or unnecessary presentation or panel examples, intimidation, stalking or following photographing or recording someone without their permission sustained disruption of talks or other events uninvited physical contact including uninvited sexual attention. Participants asked to stop any harassing behavior are expected to comply immediately. This includes not only anyone involved in the incident, but any onlookers contributing to the disruption.

WHAT ARE SOME EXAMPLES?

As a general rule, practicing common sense in physical and social interactions with strangers will ensure everyone has a comfortable convention experience. Here are some guidelines for types of behavior that may make others uncomfortable or be considered harassment.

Physically touching or endangering other people without an express invitation is never acceptable. Touching other people's personal effects without an express invitation. This includes clothing, assistive devices, bags, and on-duty service animals. If physical contact is wished, do so verbally or with a friendly gesture. Holding a hand out for a handshake is a good example.

Sharing space with other people requires active demonstrations of respect and empathy. Good examples can be: leaving other people a clear path to an exit, moderating the volume of your voice, limiting the expansiveness of your gestures as well as maintaining an appropriate physical distance.

Please respect the desires of a person or persons who have expressed their wish for no further contact. Do not contact them, either by your own agency or through an intermediary.

StokerCon® welcomes vigorous debate, but that do not verbally attack people.

Be aware of consent to continue interaction with another person, observing non-verbal and verbal clues.

Pay attention if the other party wishes to end the interaction. If there is any question if the other party wants to end the interaction, end the interaction yourself.

When in doubt, don't make assumptions: ask.

WHO CAN REPORT A PROBLEM?

Anyone who was directly affected by or witnessed harassment can file a report, and is encouraged to do so.

WHAT SHOULD I DO IF I AM BEING HARASSED?

In some cases, you may find the harassment stops if you clearly say 'no' or 'please leave me alone,' or simply walk away. We would appreciate it if a volunteer was still informed to help us identify any repeat offenders.

If you continue to be harassed or notice someone else being harassed, please contact a convention volunteer immediately. The volunteers will help participants contact venue security or law enforcement, provide escorts, or otherwise assist those experiencing harassment to feel safe during the con. The first convention volunteer or organizer you report to will take whatever steps they can to assist you in feeling safe, and will put you in contact with or bring you to an appropriate senior staff member. We value your attendance.

You do not have to give us details of the harassment and can choose whether or not to take a formal report. If you wish to report, we will take details of the harassment and work with you to respond to the issue in a way that assists you in feeling safe and maintains the safety of the wider convention environment, as well as enforcing our anti-harassment policy. If you report a serious criminal matter, please be aware that we may be obliged to contact the police. We would however take into account any concerns you may have around involving them.

If you would like to discuss the harassment without making a report, we will help you meet with the designated on-call senior staff member. Please bear in mind that this is for informal emotional support only: our volunteers don't have counselling training, and we can't promise confidentiality. You can access this service by contacting any convention volunteer.

WHAT SORT OF PROBLEM CAN I REPORT?

Any behavior or pattern of behavior that you feel comes under the definition of harassment. If you feel someone's behavior is dangerous or harmful to you or others, if someone's behavior makes you feel afraid or very uncomfortable, or if someone is actively making it difficult for you or others to enjoy or fully participate in the convention, we would like to know about it.

WHO CAN I MAKE A REPORT ABOUT?

Anyone whose behavior causes you concern. We will give all reports equal consideration. Our handling of reports will not be influenced by factors such as the social status or convention role of anyone involved in the situation.

WHEN CAN I REPORT A PROBLEM?

At any time; however, we request that reporting take place as soon as possible during or after an incident, especially if you believe that someone may be causing problems for multiple people at the convention. Reports will be taken seriously and handled appropriately regardless of when they are made.

HOW DO I FIND A CONVENTION VOLUNTEER?

Our convention volunteers are called Red Shirts and can be easily identified by their red T-Shirts. Any one of them can be your first point of contact. The volunteer may need to involve a more senior staff member to assist with your issue.

WHAT ACTIONS CAN CONVENTION STAFF
TAKE TO A HARASSMENT INCIDENT?

Senior staff reserve the right to take any action they deem appropriate, including:

- Issuing the offender with a warning if, in the determination of senior staff and/or the person reporting the Incident, the incident is considered accidental or minor;
- Making an internal note of the incident to document repeat offending;
- Making a formal report of the incident available to volunteers, senior staff or all convention participants at the discretion of senior staff; contacting hotel security; contacting law enforcement; removing the offender from the convention with no refund; and
- Reporting the offender's behavior to other convention or regulatory organizations.

If you email a report in after the convention, the Chair of StokerCon® will receive your report. They will explain in detail what the possible outcomes are and what will be asked of you, read your report, and interview other people (witnesses, the person the report is about) as necessary. The Chair will determine whether any action needs to be taken. You will be informed of any action that StokerCon® takes in connection with your report.

StokerCon® representatives will follow this policy and the internal procedures of the hotel/venue with the safety of all the convention's attendees in mind, which may require us to take certain actions without the consent of the person making the report. We will do our very best to balance the needs of all involved parties and the needs of the convention when they conflict.

WHAT WON'T HAPPEN IF I MAKE A REPORT?

We will not reveal your identity or the substance of your report unless it is absolutely necessary to obtain information about the incident or take action related to the incident.

We will not take any sort of retaliatory action against you for reporting or not reporting a problem.

We will not provide mediation or intermediary communication services.

While we will always err on the side of safety and treat all reports as true, we will not assume that a report being made automatically means that action needs to be taken.

What will happen if someone says I caused a problem?

If someone tells us that you have violated the code of conduct, two convention representatives will ask to speak with you about it in a private place.

If you decline to be interviewed, we may ask you to leave the convention. If, after speaking with you, we believe that you have acted in a manner deemed as harassment then we may ask you to change your behavior or leave the convention, or take other actions.

We will not take action until we've spoken with you and anyone else involved and done our best to get a clear picture of what happened.

If we believe that no violation occurred, you are welcome to go about the convention as usual. We will not attempt to mediate or carry messages between you and the person who made the StokerCon® report. If someone deliberately makes a false report about you, that is itself harassment and we will take appropriate action in response.

How can I help make StokerCon® safer?

Be aware of this harassment policy, of using non-oppressive language, and of boundaries.

Back up others – if you see someone being harassed or appearing uncomfortable, ask if they're okay.

OMICRON, DELTA, AND CONVENTIONS...OH MY!
A Foreword from the Co-Chairs

Three years have passed since our last in-person StokerCon®. Back then, we gathered in Grand Rapids to celebrate our work, our friendships, and our shared love of all things scary. Amid the laughs and the fun (and the ice cream!) who could have imagined the real horror would emerge a few months later and take the lives of millions of people.

It's hard to believe anyone reading this hasn't been touched in some terrible way by the COVID-19 pandemic. But the wonderful thought is you *are* reading this, which means you made it. You survived. And for that, we are truly grateful. The world has lived with too much darkness. It's refreshing to see some light.

When the pandemic forced StokerCon® to go virtual in 2021, we learned several important lessons. One, COVID-19 hadn't dampened the appetite among horror writers, readers, editors, academics, publishers, and other professionals to get together and celebrate our genre. Two, horror writers are a resilient and dedicated bunch; they made the transition to the HWA's first-ever "cybercon" as if we'd been doing it for years. Third, and perhaps most important, we learned how deeply connected we are as a community and how much we value those connections. That became obvious when we realized our virtual "hangout bars" were the most popular feature of StokerCon® 2021. What people wanted most was the opportunity to catch up with old friends, make new ones, and talk shop.

One of our fondest memories of StokerCon® 2021 was logging on first thing in the morning, each with a cup of coffee in hand, only to find friends and colleagues in Australia, New Zealand, and the United Kingdom online and eager to chat. Then as the hour grew late in their time zones, they signed off, and others signed on, an experience that mimicked a day at a real-life convention more than we ever thought it would. But the wish to really be there in person, to sit face-to-face with our colleagues and friends, never diminished.

Now, after years apart, our Ka-Tet has reformed. We've been drawn to Denver by our common purpose. Here you will find workshops and readings, presentations and panels, a film festival, celebrations, a banquet, and, of course, the Bram Stoker Awards®. All of these will circle around the heart of horror the way planets circle around a star. And you get to be part of it.

Excitement is running high. The StokerCon® 2022 committee, one of the most dedicated groups we've ever had the honor and pleasure to work with, has pulled out all the stops to make this convention as memorable an experience as possible. We're confident that in between panels and author readings, workshops and presentations, pitch sessions and ceremonies, you'll find plenty of opportunity to reconnect with old friends, make new ones, and reenergize the bonds that hold the horror community together.

We started planning this gathering in June of 2020. We're glad to finally be here.

We're glad you made it too.

Enjoy your StokerCon®!

JAMES CHAMBERS and BRIAN W. MATTHEWS
Co-Chairs
StokerCon® 2022

THE NEW FACES OF THE HWA

A Letter from the President

They say when you're in a leadership position to surround yourself with people smarter than you. That's been a priority from day one. Going hand in hand with having lots of truly brilliant people in the HWA, I've always felt having new voices is just as important. I like to tell people I grew up with a generation where having a wide variety of people was just normal and cool. Prince and the Revolution were a huge influence on me. I saw all the types of kids in my neighborhood represented up there on screen when we all went to see *Purple Rain*. Meanwhile, on MTV, we had gender benders like Boy George and Annie Lennox. We watched Bruce Springsteen give a huge soul kiss to Clarence Clemmons. We didn't think twice about it. All good. All cool. All wonderful. Meanwhile, the literary world told us stories exploring so many different lifestyles. Clive Barker's *Books of Blood* set off a literary revolution all its own. Anne Rice's lyrical vampire mythos shed light on so many exploratory paths. Poppy Z. Brite's works illuminated lifestyles that hadn't really been explored in mainstream fiction.

All of these influences have helped me pilot the HWA. As many of you may know, I don't really dig the term 'President' to describe myself. It's got so many negative connotations these days. I feel much more like a ship's captain. As someone who's spent a lot of time on boats, that analogy feels like a much better fit. Yeah, I'm at the wheel, but it takes an amazing crew to really keep a ship running well. The HWA crew are phenomenal.

We're seeing unprecedented growth in our membership and reach. For the first time, we're nearing 2,000 members. By the time this is in print, I'm sure we'll have surpassed that. Easily. With that growth we've needed to call on our volunteers to fulfill so much more need. A great example is our social media team. For years, Meghan Arcuri was doing all of it. By herself. We realized she needed help, so we brought in Sumiko Saulson, who has managed a team with Lindy Ryan, Gabrielle Faust, Jeff Oliver, Patrick Freivald, Andrew Wolter, and Micah Castle, each heading a different platform. We've grown our Membership Team, too. Carina Bissett has done an extraordinary job and created such a high standard. Roni Stinger is taking over, and is already an invaluable addition.

Our chapters grow worldwide, with new groups in India, the UK, Ireland, Romania, New Zealand and Canada, and it's wonderful to experience. It's a testament to what the HWA offers. And this is the most important part: we offer what our volunteers bring and have to give. They're the faces of the HWA. Most of our new initiatives have started and have been implemented by them. Our diversity celebrations came from Sumiko and our social media team. New scholarships have been pitched and implemented by several members. Our new Wellness Initiative was thought up and run by Ace Antonio Hall, Lee Murray, and Dave Jeffries, with a big assist from several other members. Becky Spratford and Konrad Stump are doing so much with our Library Committee. I could take up several pages. This is the HWA. Our people, helping our people. This is your HWA. Let's go crazy!

JOHN PALISANO
President
Horror Writers Association

KEVIN J. WETMORE JR.
Bram Stoker Awards® Emcee

Kevin J. Wetmore, Jr. is the two-time Stoker Award finalist for non-fiction for *The Streaming of Hill House* and *Uncovering Stranger Things,* as well as the author of over two dozen books, including *Post-9/11 Horror in American Cinema, Back from the Dead: Reading Remakes of Romero's Zombie Films as Markers of Their Times,* and *Eaters of the Dead: Myths and Realities of Cannibal Monsters.* He has also published over three dozen short stories as well, including the Lovecraft/Judy Blume mashups "Tales of a Fourth Grade Shoggoth" and "Are You There, Azathoth? It's Me, Margaret," the Pushcart Prize-nominated "Machiavelli's *The Little Prince,*" and the award-winning "The Eleventh Whale." He is also a professor at Loyola Marymount University, an actor, a stand up comic, a stage combat choreographer, an Aquarius, a loving father, doting husband, and a hell of a dancer. He serves as the co-chair of HWA Los Angeles Chapter. You can check out his work at www.SomethingWetmoreThisWayComes.com

LINDA D. ADDISON
Bram Stoker Awards® Keynote Speaker

LINDA D. ADDISON, award-winning author of five collections, including *How to Recognize a Demon Has Become Your Friend,* the first African-American recipient of the HWA Bram Stoker Award®, the HWA Lifetime Achievement Award and SFPA Grand Master of Fantastic Poetry. Her site: www.LindaAddisonWriter.com.

StokerCon

Guests of Honor

ERNEST DICKERSON

GEMMA FILES

BRIAN KEENE

JOHN EDWARD LAWSON

JENNIFER McMAHON

SHEREE RENÉE THOMAS

ERNEST DICKERSON
StokerCon® 2022 Guest of Honor

Ernest Dickerson is an Emmy, Peabody, and two-time Image Award winning film and television veteran whose signature brand of visual story-telling has been entertaining movie and TV fans for more than thirty years. Dickerson's extensive work on the silver screen and on television has successfully solidified him as one of Hollywood's top creative talents.

A native of Newark, New Jersey, Dickerson earned his undergraduate degree from Howard University, after which he attended New York University's Tisch School of the Arts. There Dickerson met filmmaker Spike Lee, with whom he would ultimately collaborate as Director of Photography on such classic films as *She's Gotta Have It*, *School Daze*, *Do the Right Thing*, *Mo' Better Blues*, and *Malcolm X*.

Dickerson's 1992 feature directorial debut *Juice*—an urban drama whose social and cultural resonance continues to this day, and which launched the film careers of Tupac Shakur and Omar Epps—gave way to other big screen credits, such as *Surviving the Game*, *Tales from the Crypt*: *Demon Knight*, *Bones* and *Never Die Alone*. His work as a visionary filmmaker and storyteller has been showcased in some of the top television shows of the past decade, including hit series like *"The Wire," "The Walking Dead," "Treme," "Dexter," "Heroes," "Weeds,"* and many others.

Some of Dickerson's most recent television credits includes the 2022 premier of HBO's *"Raised By Wolves"* along with *"DMZ"* and *"Interrogation"* where he also served as Executive Producer on both, Amazon's *"Bosch"* and *"The Man In The High Castle,"* Netflix's *"House of Cards"* and *"Seven Seconds"* and Epix's hit series *"Godfather of Harlem."* Dickerson's independent feature, *Double Play,* based on the internationally acclaimed Frank Martinus Arion novel and filmed on the island of Curacao, will be available for streaming in early 2022.

Dickerson, who is a long-standing member of the Directors Guild of America (DGA) and the American Society of Cinematographers (ASC), currently resides in Los Angeles, California.

A CONVERSATION WITH ERNEST DICKERSON
by Jonathan Lees

JONATHAN LEES (JL): Let's kick it off. I could sit here and speak to you for hours regarding your work as a cinematographer and everything in and around your career, which is extremely extensive, but there's one thing I wanted to know upfront: you worked as a medical photographer at Howard University medical school for a couple of years, did this inform your love of the macabre? Or, was there something more informative that started earlier?

ERNEST DICKERSON (ED): It started a lot earlier. I grew up with a love of the macabre. The earliest movie I can ever remember seeing was a movie about a giant octopus that destroyed the Golden Gate Bridge, a Ray Harryhausen film. I saw that at the movies when I was young. I was probably around four years old.

JL: That was *It Came from Beneath the Sea*, right?

ED: That's it. And, you know, growing up we always went to see scary movies. I went to see movies like *The Tingler, I Was Teenage Frankenstein, House on Haunted Hill,* the original *House on Haunted Hill.* I remember a movie that scared the living daylights out of me, Roger Corman's *The Pit and the Pendulum,* and just seeing good horror films. Saturday nights you always had creature features. Saturday night was always devoted to seeing a couple of horror films. I'd do that with my friends. We'd make popcorn and we'd make burgers. Just stay up and watch scary movies. So, I grew up on a lot of Roger Corman films and a lot of Mario Bava films, ones that they started showing on television. And I've been a reader. I started reading science fiction first. I got more into horror when I was in high school.

And when I discovered the writings of H.P. Lovecraft that really kind of blew me away.

JL: What was it about those texts that drew you in? Lovecraft is very image forward and, as an image maker, that kind of makes sense to me.

ED: Well, the atmosphere in his stories just never went away. You know, they just creeped me out. Those really hit me, and actually for a Christmas present, one Christmas, I got the book *Dracula* by Bram Stoker. I think I was probably around ten or eleven years old. And reading that scared the living daylights out of me. That was a scary book.

JL: What did you connect to emotionally?

ED: I think it was, again, it was the atmosphere. It was the first person narratives which gave it a level of reality like somebody had actually experienced it. But you know, the images in there, Jonathan Harker being trapped in Dracula's castle and looking out the window and seeing him climbing down the wall. I said 'Whoa, wait a minute. Bela Lugosi never did that.'

They gave me a whole other appreciation of Dracula as a character. The first Dracula that I ever saw was Bela Lugosi for the Universal films and I grew up seeing the Universal horror films, you know, the Frankensteins, *The Creature from the Black Lagoon.*

So, by the time I got into medical photography I was already looking at horror films and the guys that I was working with in the photography section they were movie buffs. So, we would go see a lot of movies in Washington, D.C. that had a great repertory theater showing classic films, you know midnight movies. That's when I first saw *Eraserhead,* when I was living in

D.C. and that blew me away, *The Rocky Horror Picture Show,* and the AFI always had great screenings. I could say that the macabre has been in my life since the beginning.

JL: I love that you brought up Mario Bava only because you have, from the get-go, whether it was working with Spike Lee or DP'ing *Brother from Another Planet*, a great sense of color, richness and movement, and even though those weren't horror films, sometimes the staging felt like you were there with the emotion of the characters. Did you learn any of that from horror, do you think?

ED: I think I probably did learn it from horror. I mean, you look at stuff and it impacts on your personality somehow. Absorbing a lot of stuff, seeing a lot of movies because it wasn't just horror films that was affecting me. In film school, I was affected by a lot of Italian films, you know, other Italian films other than Bava, or the cinematography of Vittorio Storaro. But also seeing movies like *Apocalypse Now* and just appreciating them and being also a fan of Hitchcock in high school. The first film that I ever saw of Hitchcock that really drew me to Hitchock was *Vertigo*. And to this day it's still one of my favorite films and that's a slightly macabre piece of work too. So, all these different movies they all, I think, contributed.

JL: And before you became confident enough to break from behind the camera to direct, some of the things that might've informed your work on *Tales from the Crypt: Demon Knight* was possibly that you were the director of photography on a whole lot of *Tales from the Darkside* episodes in the eighties. Did the work on *Tales from the Darkside* give you the confidence for that level of very specific tone, a blending of horror and humor?

ED: Yeah. The great thing about *Tales from the Darkside* being an anthology show, every episode I felt should have its own look. And, so, I always tried to visually treat each episode differently. It gave me a chance to experiment with different types of lighting, different effects, different ways of achieving atmosphere and stuff like that. And then *Tales from the Darkside* got me a job as second unit cinematographer on *Day of the Dead*. I went down and shot a couple of days in Florida on *Day of the Dead*. There is a whole opening sequence which shows how civilization has been totally disrupted; like an alligator sitting on top of the piles of money in front of a bank, just the empty streets and the newspaper saying the dead have risen.

Shooting all that and doing that on a budget, because it was not an expensive film and second unit work, we definitely didn't have a lot of stuff. So, we had to be very specific in what images we saw and what we didn't see. And that's where I first met Greg Nicotero.

JL: Then fast forward into the future and you're directing episodes of *The Walking Dead*.

ED: Yeah.

JL: Well, let's not move too fast. After *Juice*, you worked on *Tales from the Crypt* and this was such a bizarre period of time for horror: the mid-nineties. This was a year before *Scream* changed the language of horror films, but here you were working off a very successful HBO television show. *Demon Knight* was a mid-nineties film that I felt had the spirit of the mid-to-late eighties, but also based on a fifties comic book. So, it's a lot of work to get all those tones in, but there's so much humor and so much energy that I feel like might've been informed by some of the greats, like, *Evil Dead*, and Peter Jackson with *Bad Taste* and *Dead Alive*.

Did you have sort of trepidation walking into a property that was so well loved? Not only from like decades before in comic books, but also off a hit series. How did you get into that project and what was like your core focus going in as a director?

ED: The interesting thing about it is in the script stage, it didn't start out as a *Tales from the Crypt* film.

It started out as an independent horror film. The producers just decided to use that script to be the first of the movies of the *Tales from the Crypt*. It doesn't follow the typical *Tales from the Crypt* format which is usually kind of like a comeuppance tale, but this was a totally different piece of work. I approached it as a horror film and I got it right after I finished doing *Surviving the Game.* That's what got me the job.

I was just trying to make the best horror film I could. It was people trapped in a house and how are they going to get out of it. And it all takes place in one night. It was a lot of fun working a lot of that stuff out. The film I was probably looking at a lot was *Aliens*, just in terms of the alien attack. And, you know, being a student of low-budget techniques that James Cameron brought to that film and the stuff that he did in the Roger Corman days, that helped inform some of the decisions I had to make in doing *Demon Knight.*

JL: You were bringing this VHS vibe to the multiplex. It was a tone we were not familiar with in your work. How difficult was it for you to ground that comedy, the timing?

ED: You know, it just felt right. With Billy Zane, working out the character of The Collector, we wanted him to have this irreverent attitude towards human beings, these meat puppet type people, and his utter disdain for them. Like when he calls them a bunch of ho-dunk, po-dunk, well them there motherfuckers. That was Billy having fun with it, and we did that, alternating between the seriousness and him just bending his anger in some pretty funny ways at these puny human beings that are keeping him from getting his key, which is what he really wants.

JL: Yeah, man. Well, with all that power comes cockiness.

ED: And we had a really comfortable situation shooting too. I think we shot it in like in thirty days. I did not want to be shooting thirty nights out in the desert. And, so, I really pushed for trying to find some way of doing it, building a countryside indoors. We finally found a decommissioned airplane hangar at Van Nuys Airport. And that's where we built everything. And everybody got to go home at the end of the day.

It was more comfortable and more controlled that way. So, the pressure wasn't as great as it could have been. I just knew that, you know, we were shooting all nights. That's the worst thing you can do to a crew, that we would have reached the point of no return, diminishing returns.

JL: I thought it was interesting, considering the time, Jada Pinkett was given the chance for a lead role. Is this something you actively fought for?

ED: Yeah. I had just seen her in *Menace II Society* and I wanted somebody small for Jeryline you know? I was hoping I could find an African-American because I thought, well, she's gonna wind up being the last lady standing. Black people are gonna think that, you know, she's gonna die, you know, she's going to be one of the first to go.

Because that's usually what happens in horror; any person of color is usually the first person to get killed. But when I saw her in *Menace II Society*, I said, 'Yo, that's her. That's my Jeryline.' And I met with her. And then I had to sell her to Joel Silver and because Joel had another idea in mind, but Jada went in and talked to him and impressed him.

JL: I love it. I'm glad that they gave you the opportunity to pick someone who really shined and would normally not get the role of the final girl. What you did next with *Bones* is you created something entirely playing off their off-screen persona, as a hip-hop artist, and also their personality, which is Snoop Dogg. Creating Bones for him, was that a collaboration?

ED: Yeah, well, it always is. At least in the way that I work. I believe that old adage, that 85% to 90% of directing is casting and Snoop just has this personality.

He was basically playing himself but he had that gravitas and he took it quite seriously. He was a total joy to work with. He loved the character of Jimmy Bones and you know, it was amazing to see Snoop blush kissing Pam Grier because he had grown up falling in love with Pam Grier like so many of us did, and now that I have put them in a position where you kiss her and hold her and hug her. It made Snoop and me friends for life because of that. [Laughs]

He took it quite seriously He was really into creating this tragic character.

JL: We don't often see what would be considered a real *urban* legend, as in based in a city. They're usually *suburban* legends. How important was it for you to bring like an inner city vibe and a feel which you've already explored quite well in films like *Juice*, but what was it specific to this film that just made it feel more special to have that connection to the city?

ED: Well, I grew up in an inner city. I grew up in Newark, New Jersey.

JL: Jersey!

ED: Oh, you're from Jersey too?

JL: I'm from Massachusetts originally, but I live in Jersey currently.

ED: I grew up in Newark. I lived in a housing project until I was about eighteen. You know, horror stories of the city and urban legends, was something I grew up with.

Jimmy Bones was conceived as a gentleman gangster [in the 1970s], a man who took care of his neighborhood, a man whose neighborhood was safe. You know, there were things that he would not allow to happen in there. I think his downfall with the fact that he refused to get involved in the drug trade there. And so, you know, bringing that to life and finding that place that we could also advance into the modern day where he's dead.

Lookwise, I was really channeling Bava in that film especially a film that he did called *The Whip and the Body*. The cinematography of that film gets very, very dark, daringly dark for a movie from the early sixties. And so, a lot of the feelings in that film really stayed in my head when I was making films. There was a love story there too, [one] I think everybody that's lost somebody they loved would love to have. You know what if you have the chance of somebody you love coming back from the dead, but they might not come back the way you remember them.

JL: I think that's what's fun about these films is that it feels like there's so much that you want to do with every project you take on. Like, it feels like all these influences from your life, your childhood and your love for cinema, everything's bleeding through.

I just picture you as the child, in *Demon Knight,* when the eyes pop out of the frame of his comic book, that's Ernest Dickerson. [Laughs]

Did anything change for you when you started working in TV? *The Wire*, *Bosch*, working with Mick Garris on *Masters of Horror, The V Word, Dexter, The Purge, Damien, Walking Dead*. I mean, for you, as someone who had such control over the visual element in the early stages of your career, to someone who established more control as the director of projects... I've heard often when you step into TV, you're in someone else's universe, with a cast of characters that may have already done twenty episodes. How do you work in that environment in comparison to all the stuff you've done before?

ED: I mean, that is one of the things that I do miss, and now I'm trying to take on projects where I do have a more creative part. I was fortunate enough to work in the first season of *Walking Dead*. And then I worked on, I think, five seasons of the show. They gave me some major episodes where I basically storyboarded the whole thing. And that was my way of maintaining control which really helped with these really tight schedules the show had.

The first big one I had, with the second season finale, which was the attack on Hershel's farm, was a massive undertaking. Normally, the shows were done in eight days and they gave me one extra day for that. And, it was cold, November in Georgia can get pretty brutal. I storyboarded the whole thing so that I knew what was going to happen and when. And that's something that I had done with all the other episodes, all the attacks in the prison, you know, things that need design.

I did the first episode going into the prison, which gave the show another environment and another look. The script didn't get exact in how they went in. How these few people were going to go in and protect themselves from the zombies. And I remember when I took Latin in high school, talking about how the Romans used to do a thing called a phalanx, where they go in all together, back-to-back, so everybody's looking out, so whichever way the enemy is coming at you, you can fight them off. And so, I designed that whole trip when they go inside, how they get through the place, like a military operation, like a phalanx.

Zombies coming from this way. You go and you'd kill it. Then you get back up, zombies coming in that way. 'Cause you didn't know which direction they were going to be coming.

JL: I love that they give you one of the most intense episodes. And then one of the most emotionally draining episodes. I can't imagine stepping into a project where you're handed the two crux moments of the season.

ED: What was really interesting with that I became really good friends with Scott Wilson and he actually moved about a five-minute drive from me. Outside of the *Walking Dead*, he was my bourbon drinking and cigar smoking buddy. We would get together because he was just such a wonderful guy and we're still really tight with his widow, with his wife, who we see all the time. I introduced his character. I burnt down his farm. I chopped off his leg in the first episode of the third season. And I wound up chopping off his head. I directed the one where the Governor chopped off his head.

And when I first read the script I was like oh noooooo...

JL: Devastating.

ED: You know, he was a totally professional actor. He was so cool. And he said, hey, that's why it's written this way. It's gotta be so.

JL: On these shows, it must be hard to walk in, form the relationship, then walk out. Is there something that you haven't done yet that you're just like, man, I gotta do this. It's got to happen. What's the dream project?

ED: Well, actually, you know, we're still in touch with a lot of the people, you know, my wife has these undead zoom calls, you know, we get together, we get whoever's available, Gale Anne Hurd, Danai Gurira, Scott Gimple, maybe like once a month, we'll have these zoom calls where everybody will get on and just catch up.

And sometimes we'll all have dinner together. So, and the same thing with *The Wire,* stayed friends with a lot of people in *The Wire*. Sonja Sohn and my wife are best friends. Jamie Hector who played Marlo was best man at my wedding, Chad Coleman, Andre Royal, we're still all in touch with each other. We've made some really honest-to-goodness friendships and still stay in touch with a lot of people. But in terms of what I'm hoping to do, well, I'm writing. I'm definitely writing and I'm hoping to get some of that made. I recently was able to do a show that was really a lot of fun. I did the first two episodes of the second season of *Raised by Wolves*, which is a show that's set on the planet Kepler-22b. And right after that I did another show called *DMZ* which is set in New York after a 21st century civil war, kinda like a little bit of *Escape from New York* meets *The Warriors*.

JL: Is that based on the comic book?

ED: Yes, on the DC graphic novel.

JL: Nice! That's fantastic. The stuff that you're writing is it almost always script based or do you dabble in fiction?

ED: I've been writing scripts. My wife and I wrote a horror film where some people might want to turn into a series. It's called *No Face* and it's surgical horror. I wrote another show adapting Edgar Allan Poe to modern day, and there's a very famous science fiction novel that I'm involved in. I don't think I can talk about it just yet, but a very famous science fiction novel by a famous author that we're kind of in the early stages of development now. And you know, always just looking for good material, reading different books. I have a lot of fantastic fiction up there.

JL: Are there any modern authors that are really driving you nuts? Like someone that you have to go back to and read everything they do? Or is it, are you diversifying and trying to find little pockets of horror fiction that's out there now or genre fiction, period?

ED: Yeah, really, you know, kind of like looking around diversifying. I'm really interested in cosmic horror. Because I think that's where Lovecraft, where his main thing came from, the horror of the unknown and to me, that's what is the scariest thing that we have going. The unknown, the cosmos, you know, things in the universe we can't know about or explain. I'm always looking for good material.

JL: Is there any book in mind that you've read recently in cosmic horror that you really just went for?

ED: I read something called *The Deep* by Nick Cutter, which is an interesting book. I'm always looking. I'm always trying to find something that's doable.

JL: If you haven't read Laird Barron, Victor LaValle...major.

Ernest Dickerson: *The Ballad of Black Tom* is an amazing book. I love how he just completely subverted the racism in Lovecraft's story.

That was one of the things about loving Lovecraft's writing, being a man of color, one of the things I had to deal with was the racism and that story. I love how some of the authors are taking it and twisting it around like LaValle did and like in the book *Lovecraft Country*. I read that book and as soon as I read it I was like 'Ooh. Wow. What's up with the rights to this?' but they had already been snatched up, but there are other books out there that I'm looking at. There's a couple of books I'm trying to find out the rights situation on. Always looking for new material.

JL: Is there a property, a franchise that you loved growing up that you would love to be a part of re-imagining?

ED: I've got to think about that. Right off the top of my head no. I've always tried to find something new. I can't think of anything right now. I've started looking at a lot of older stuff again. Like the original series *Thriller* hosted by Boris Karloff. My wife and I just binged watched the first season. We're going to get into the second season, but those were great. I'd love to see those come back, you know? It's interesting because I showed a couple episodes of some friends of mine who weren't hip to anthology, the idea of an anthology series. It was a new concept to them. They hadn't even seen shows like *Black Mirror* but you know, anthology shows are great and I'd love to see them come back. And looking at *Thriller* this show came out when I was ten years old and some of this stuff's pretty strong. I mean, it's pretty creepy stuff. Really well-done horror for television. It didn't hold back.

JL: I would really love to see something come back that strong that allowed a lot of fresh voices to speak to the language of horror and to, you know, like just what you were talking about working on the anthology shows of the past *Tales from the Darkside* and then eventually some of the series you worked on. It's like there's a lot of talent, with the fiction that's being told, there's a lot of talent behind the camera and here an anthology show is the way you can showcase so many voices, so many perspectives.

I'd want you to do it. Next up!

ED: I'd love to.

GEMMA FILES
StokerCon® 2022 Guest of Honor

Formerly a film critic, journalist, screenwriter and teacher, GEMMA FILES has been an award-winning horror author since 1999. She has published four collections of short work, three collections of speculative poetry, a Weird Western trilogy, a story-cycle and a stand-alone novel (*Experimental Film*, which won the 2015 Shirley Jackson Award for Best Novel and the 2016 Sunburst Award for Best Adult Novel). She has a new story collection just out from Grimscribe Press (*In That Endlessness, Our End*), and another upcoming (*Dark Is Better*, from Trepidatio).

THE SANGUINTALIST

by Gemma Files

And the Name said unto Cain, Thy brother's blood cries out to me from the ground.

I wake up covered in blood, but it's not mine; I wake up covered in blood, and it *is* mine. Six of one, half-dozen of the other—take your pick. This is the world I live in and always has been.

I am a forensic necromancer for hire, of a very specific kind. Some of us work with flesh, some with bone, some with what flesh and bone leave behind. I once knew a woman who chased memories along their neural pathways, those electrochemical ghosts that can live on for days inside a corpse, even when its human topsoil is already being furrowed by insects looking for somewhere warm(ish) and easily permeable to lay their eggs, a field their children can eat their way free of. Her gift was a hard one, easy to mangle and misconstrue, like braiding tissue paper. Eventually, she ended up with a headful of other people's voices and a datebook full of the sort fragile people should best avoid for fear of getting the pixie-dust rubbed off their little wings. I'm not entirely sure what happened to her, in the end, but I do keep my eye out for any trace of her, lit or fig.

GEMMA FILES

For myself, I work with the red stuff. It's my calling. And easier by far than so many other things, given the relatively short window of its particular half-life. Accidents and murders, that's my meat: a short stop, a sudden drop, a spatter, or a pool. By the time it's dry, it locks me back out, mostly. Or so I tell my customers.

They don't need to know everything about you, after all, not when your relationship's purely business.

So I'm out picking up dinner, and my phone buzzes: ARSEHOLE NUMBER TEN, it says, because you need to be specific. Number Ten's name is Satyamurthy. Murder Squad when he's at home, and even when he's not.

I sigh, thumb working. *What you want?* the blinking text asks him.

Another buzz. *You, obviously. Here.* And an address.

I'm eating.

Do it fast, then. The cursor rests, then: *You might regret it.*

You might be surprised.

I inhale my curry, then I'm off. The site's not exactly walkable, but I grab a cab pretty easy. They don't send cars for you, more's the pity; don't want your name on the record.

Satyamurthy's outside, impatient, waiting to wave me in. His partner, Colville, turns around quick-time as I enter, hand almost twitching in the direction of that gun they're neither of them supposed to have.

"Don't step on the evidence," she barks.

"Try my best," I reply. It's a challenge, all right—stuff is everywhere you look, splashed up high, probably from carotid *and* jugular at once, given how wide the corpse's second mouth gapes. But she knows that.

The body's nude and basically faceless. Looks like someone did it with a brick? Everything's all mushed up, red stuck with shards, shattered bone bristles, the occasional tooth; hands are gone at the wrists, possibly for time's sake, dumped somewhere they'll end up similarly deconstructed. If it weren't for the dick, lying snug and slack up against one gore-smeared thigh...ah, but that doesn't always mean much, does it? Or less than it used to, anyhow, as I should know.

"You want a name, I take it?" I ask Satyamurthy, not looking up to watch him nod. Because my gaze is all on this one, now—that blank ruin, equally dented all over, only a rough geographic idea left to tell you where the eye-sockets should go. Yet there's a pull to it nevertheless, a sort of gravity; I can feel it, even from here. It's telling me bend down, get closer, ask my questions. It's telling me it *wants* to tell me, so come meet it halfway, before its time runs out. Before the blood it's still trying to shed finally goes cold.

You damn well wait your turn, I warn it, as I do.

So: down on my haunches, a deep squat, arse to heels. I rummage through my pockets, slipping on my thumb-rings—antique bone, fossilized, worn so thin with use my skin tints them from the inside. Iron reinforcements so they don't break under pressure, with sharpened horn set in a deep groove across my knuckles: right, left, curved like beaks, points extending well past my nails. Set them to the pads of my forefingers and they dent the skin; no scar tissue, see? I don't have to break the skin to draw blood, never have.

Not when it comes when I call it.

Cruentation, that's the old term—blood evidence. Bring a corpse with traces of violence into the presence of its suspected murderer and watch to see if it starts to bleed. Root of the word comes from the Latin, *cruentare,* to make bloody, and they really did use to not only pull that whole rigamarole but also bring it up in court afterwards, way back before proper forensics. Back when the intersection of maths, physics and biology, alchemy, religion, and magic was a sight more slippery than it is today, and the same people who'd just learned you could see little bugs swimming around in a drop of water under a microscope's lens still thought women's wombs wandered around their bodies, getting all clogged with rotten sperm and producing fumes that made them go hysterical.

My blood to yours, then, and your blood to mine—cry out, make your plea, your last appeal. I'll help you, if I can; justice isn't always possible, but I'll try my best. Hear you and remember from now on, either way.

This promise is an old one, older than old. My mother taught it to me, like hers taught her. It goes back forever.

We were priests and kings once, Lala, my little one, my Nani used to tell me, and still does, even when I don't want to listen. *Long before Kukkutarma became Mohenjo-daro, for all its name reflects our former glory. Before the glaciers grew and retreated, even, in the very morning of the world, when everything was equally unstable. When all our cities were graves, and all our graves cities.*

(Yes, yes. But this ain't then, is it? And I'm on the clock and time is money, theoretical square root of this whole bloody late-stage capitalism barter system. I scratch Satya's back, he scratches mine ...)

That's how it should go, anyway; almost always does. Even if we don't often itch in *quite* the same places, him and me.

I close my eyes, feeling my fingertips pink and bruise as the drops start forming: all that tiny life, forever swimming and fighting, eating and dividing, without rest or pity. Each globule a secret universe caught in the moment of creation, utterly unaware of its own precariousness, dim and scarlet and salt.

There's a thrum in the air when the corpse's blood recognizes mine, sparking, a struck string. A red mist rises from the body's pores, sending out feelers, and I can already hear Colville draw breath behind me, give out a disgusted little grunt. It doesn't break my concentration. I know my business better than that.

Now, I say, silent, tongue moving against my teeth, the roof of my shut mouth. *Tell me now. Show me, if you can't form the words. Let me see it.*

Let me see it all.

A CONVERSATION WITH GEMMA FILES

by Carina Bissett

Canadian author Gemma Files broke into the horror scene nearly three decades ago with the publication of her first professional short story "Fly-by-Night." Since then, her work has been regularly featured on award ballots and "Year's Best" anthologies for good reason. Dale L. Sproule at *Rue Morgue* calls her prose "terse and muscular yet highly poetic." Jeff VanderMeer lauds her as "one of the great dark imaginations in fiction—visionary, transgressive, and totally original." And Caitlin R. Kiernan says, "Boldly, brazenly, Gemma Files pushes her hands deep into the red and seeping unconscious places and finds the bits of treasure worth pulling back out into the light." Files's stories are brutal and beautiful, her novels filled with lush violence and diamond-sharp dread. Together, these transgressive treasures create an award-winning canon of work that firmly places Files at the top of her class—a master storyteller in her own right.

CARINA BISSETT (CB): Your first horror story "Fly-by-Night" came out in 1993. As you approach the thirtieth anniversary of that first publication, what advice would you give your younger self?

GEMMA FILES (GF): Don't ever be afraid to write whatever comes into your head, because there's always someone out there who'll respond to it the same way you do, or even more strongly. One of my favourite moments from the last ten years was when a young writer told me: "You wrote the story that proved I could write anything I wanted." "Oh, what was it?" I asked. "'Kissing Carrion,'" they said, proudly, thus proving that that hot second of self-doubt I had after writing a story in which a woman uses a mechanized corpse as a sex puppet in order to fuck her necrophile bf in public while the ghost of the guy who used to be that corpse floats by disapprovingly was apparently totally unnecessary.

CB: Your award-winning story "The Emperor's Old Bones" was originally published in *Northern Frights* in 1998 and was reprinted in *The Year's Best Fantasy and Horror Thirteenth Annual Collection*, edited by Terri Windling and Ellen Datlow. (Readers can also find it archived at *Nightmare Magazine*, Issue 38, November 2015.) Since that first reprint, you've been featured in numerous anthologies featuring the best of the best in horror. Do you have any advice for writers when it comes to reprints and awards?

GF: I'm always very interested in what stories get reprinted, not necessarily because I think if you study them you can figure out some way to game the system—pretty sure you can't—but because those stories might possibly give you some idea about what qualities other people think characterize your own writing, which is always useful. It also gives you a jolt of objectivity about/an exterior perspective on your own work, which can help free you from whatever rut you might have most recently gotten yourself stuck in. Plus, attention of any sort cultivates gratitude, which is good for you in general; if you end up getting an award, make sure to thank everybody you can think of, including yourself.

CB: Out of your numerous accolades, is there any one in particular that stands out for you?

GF: I'm always surprised when I get recognized for anything, so I think I'll have to go with the time my story "The Emperor's Old Bones" was nominated for a 1999 International Horror Guild award for Best Short Fiction, up against entries by Neil Gaiman and Kim Newman, and I was so convinced there was no possible way I'd win that Ed Bryant literally had to phone me and very gently suggest I really should change my mind about showing up at that year's World Horror Convention, because it just *might* be worth my while. Everything since then has been gravy.

CB: Your novel *Experimental Film* (2015) won the Shirley Jackson Award for Best Novel and the Sunburst Award for Best Canadian Speculative Fiction. Does your work in cinema continue to influence your fiction?

GF: Yes, absolutely. I'm obsessed with reproducing visuals in prose, with beating out action in much the same way a screenplay does, and (most of all) with exploring the potential of found footage narrative tropes when applied to books and stories rather than movies and TV. What are we seeing, and how, and why? From whose perspective? In what order? Who curated the documentation? Is anything being suggested liminally, present only through the holes it leaves behind after having been edited out? I don't think I'll ever get bored with applying these tactics, no matter what sort of tale I'm telling.

CB: You often talk about your work as a film critic. What is your opinion of the translation of novels to the screen and vice versa?

GF: It's really difficult to translate most novels directly to the screen, unless that screen is a small one—novels usually work far better as the inspiration for TV series/miniseries, whereas the best movie adaptations tend to come from short stories or novellas. That said, I have to give a shout-out to Brian Helgeland and Curtis Hanson's script for *L.A. Confidential*, which manages to condense a ridiculously complicated James Ellroy joint covering seven years of action into a short, sharp noir whose plot takes maybe a year to spin out. Granted, they do that by basically changing everything but the characters and the themes, but sometimes that's the challenge.

CB: More and more women are writing in the genres of horror and dark fiction. Have you seen a shift in the horror community as a result? Do you have any advice for women who feel as though they are struggling to fit in with what has been historically known as a male-dominated field?

GF: Yeah, I've definitely seen a shift, and not just in terms of more women writing horror—I love how diverse the field is getting generally, with more and more original, interesting, *different* voices joining the mix; I love the fact that half these people seem to have been here all along, being who they are, doing what they do. Nothing narrows a genre like the assumption that only certain types of people (default types, natch) should be represented, for fear of losing your audience. The fact is, every time you add a new level of perspective, a new audience is created—an audience made up of people who never thought they were going to see anyone like themselves in the sort of stories they love so much. And each new sub-audience swells the audience as a whole, so why the hell would anyone want less of that? My main advice is to talk about what you love and forget what you don't, support each other, read hungrily, write passionately, talk, edit, pitch, publish...do it all, don't think you can't. Don't EVER think you can't.

CB: You often interact with others on Twitter (weird menace and excessive bloodletting @gemmafiles) and once advised another writer that *not* writing can actually be productive, as it allows the brain to continue to work on solutions without the pressure of putting words on the page. Have you ever taken a prolonged break in your career? If so, how did it affect your writing when you came back to it?

GF: Ha, good question. I spent maybe ten years teaching in my thirties, and that really ate into my capacity to move from writing ever-expanding "short" stories to actual full-length novels; that ended in a year of depression after I lost my job and had to deal with my son's Autism Spectrum Disorder diagnosis, which I mainly spent writing nothing but *3:10 to Yuma* fanfiction. Right after that, however, I finally made the jump and parlayed all that Wild West research into the Hexslinger series. I think I'm teetering on the edge of doing something similar with my next novel(s), especially since it's been over five years since *Experimental Film*—the next leap might be from writing short stories anytime I'm asked to just because I know I can to making a genuine strategic plan and sticking to it 'til it's done. And make it pay.

CB: I love your pinned tweet: "For those who just followed me: She/her/hers, neuroatypical (Asperger's), a preliminary sketch of a crone, raised areligious, talks about film a lot/too much, poetic purple prose, firm proponent of monster pride. I try to be kind." As an advocate of neurodiversity, what would you like to see evolve in the continuing discussion about the social model of disability and divergence?

GF: More and more, I truly do believe that neurotypicality as a concept may be just as much of a lie as any other sort of "normal"/default identity. We all have our somethings; often, those somethings seem to cross back and forth over each other, forming a spectrum so wide it's more of a circle we could all find our place on, if we were only inclined to. For me, figuring out how my own brain works and why was incredibly freeing, as was accepting that being different isn't the same thing as being broken—and yes, both realizations came out of needing to connect with and advocate for my son, but I get that not everybody is lucky enough to have that particular impetus to build on. Then again, my experiences are very much generational; I'm really happy to see so many young creatives around these days who got their diagnoses early enough to be able to skip past the part where I spent twenty years wondering what the fuck was wrong with me, instead of being able to go: "Well, my brain has trouble with x, x and x...what else?"

There's just so much shame and anger involved with the process of socialization, which we ALL need, instead of empathy, which is the only really effective teaching aid. We need to be able to love and forgive ourselves, so we can love and forgive others; we need to be able to accept that no one is stronger apart, that humans *have* to learn to live with each other, because there's no other option. And storytelling is the key—storytelling, performance, music, communication. I believe that devoutly, the same way Martin Scorsese believes cinema is a secular church. The only religion that really matters is helping each other to not hate ourselves and do the things that make us feel useful. To find our own vocations.

CB: What does a typical writing session/day look like? Do you have any special habits or rituals that help you get started?

GF: These days, it's hard. My first impulse is always to go out to a coffee shop, stick on my headphones and hammer at the keyboard until my ass hurts too much to stay there anymore, but I can't do any of that right now. So, instead, I end up doing things late at night or really early in the morning, waiting until I can be as "alone" as it's possible to be in a one-bedroom apartment occupied by three full-grown humans. Coffee is important. Music is important. Sometimes I start by journaling, then transcribe notes; sometimes I just open a file and go. It depends on the deadline. I try for 500/1,000 words a day, and I try not to quibble over how I get them.

CB: In February 2021, you released your newest short story collection *In That Endlessness, Our End* with Grimscribe Press. This release is hot on the heels of the two short fiction collections you published with Trepidatio Publishing/JournalStone in 2018: *Spectral Evidence* and *Drawn Up from Deep Places*. What is your process in putting a short fiction collection together?

GF: I generally try to look for links between the stories, either in terms of content or in terms of theme, but sometimes it's as simple as "this stuff is mainly contemporary horror" vs "this stuff mainly isn't" (*Kissing Carrion* vs *The Worm in Every Heart*, as well as *SE* vs *DUFDP*). In terms of *In That Endlessness...*, meanwhile, all the stories were written either just pre- or post-Trump, and when I finally laid them next to each other, I recognized a thread of commonality that almost seemed to predict the last year and a half's slowpocalyptic existential upheaval. It'll be interesting to see what people make of my next collection, *Dark Is Better* (Trepidatio, 2022), which was assembled over a much longer time-frame and covers some of the same ground as *This Is Not For You and Others/ Esto No Es Para Vosotros y Otras Historias* (La Biblioteca de Carfax, 2021).

CB: What projects are you currently working on, and what can we expect to see coming out in the future?

GF: Three novels in the pipe, pre-pitched to a particular publisher—I want to get at least one of them done by the middle of next year. *Dark is Better*. A new collection of poetry. A collection of biographical essays about horror culture. More teaching. More talking about movies. More weird doodles. I want to die writing. Likelihood seems high.

BRIAN KEENE

StokerCon® 2022 Guest of Honor

BRIAN KEENE writes novels, comic books, short stories, and nonfiction. He is the author of over fifty books, mostly in the horror, crime, and fantasy genres. They have been translated into over a dozen different languages and have won numerous awards (see below). His 2003 novel, *The Rising,* is credited with inspiring pop culture's recurrent interest in zombies. He has also written for such media properties as *Doctor Who, Thor, Aliens, Harley Quinn, The X-Files, Doom Patrol, Justice League, Hellboy, Superman,* and *Masters of the Universe.* From 2015 to 2020, he hosted the immensely popular *The Horror Show with Brian Keene* podcast. He also hosts (along with Christopher Golden) the *Defenders Dialogue* podcast.

Several of Keene's novels and stories have been adapted for film, including *Ghoul, The Naughty List, The Ties That Bind,* and *Fast Zombies Suck.* Several more are in-development. Keene also served as Executive Producer for the feature length film *I'm Dreaming of a White Doomsday.* Keene's work has been praised by the *New York Times, The History Channel, The Howard Stern Show, CNN,* the *Huffington Post, Bleeding Cool, Publisher's Weekly, Fangoria, Bloody Disgusting,* and *Rue Morgue.* Keene also serves on the Board of Directors for the Scares That Care 501c charity organization. The father of two sons, Keene lives in rural Pennsylvania with author Mary SanGiovanni.

AWARDS

Winner — 2001 Bram Stoker Award for Nonfiction (for *Jobs in Hell*)

Winner — 2003 Bram Stoker Award for First Novel (for *The Rising*)

Winner — 2004 Shocker Award for Non-Fiction Book of the Year (for *Sympathy for the Devil*)

Winner — 2014 World Horror Grandmaster Award

Winner — 2015 Imaginarium Film Festival Award for Best Screenplay, Best Short Film Genre, and Best Short Film Overall (for *I'm Dreaming of a White Doomsday*)

Winner — 2016 Imadjinn Award for Best Fantasy Novel (for *King of the Bastards*)

Winner — 2017 This Is Horror Award for Nonfiction Podcast of the Year (for *The Horror Show with Brian Keene*)

HONORS

— Whiteman A.F.B. 509th Logistics Fuels Flight (2005)

— Convergence GOH Appreciation Award (2007)

— Indiana Horror Writers Adeptus Exemptus (inducted 2008)

— Convergence GOH Appreciation Award (2009)

— Convergence GOH Appreciation Award (2011)

— United States Army International Security Assistance Force in Afghanistan (2013)

— Necon One Star Review All Stars (2014)

— Thunderstorm Books Appreciation Award (2015)

— Necon Hall of Fame (inducted 2018)

— Scares That Care President's Award (2018)

NOMINATIONS

— 2001 Bram Stoker Award nomination for Long Fiction (for *Earthworm Gods*)

— 2001 Bram Stoker Award nomination for Alternative Forms (for *Horrorfind*)

— 2001 Bram Stoker Award nomination for Anthology (for *The Best of Horrorfind*)

— 2020 Bram Stoker Award nomination for Non-Fiction (for *End of the Road*)

TOOTHPICK

by Brian Keene

This wasn't how things were supposed to turn out.

I'm not talking about the virus. We both knew that would happen again, sooner or later, and we prepared for it, same as we would for a flood or a tornado or another economic recession. I mean, we lived through the last pandemic, back when we were kids—our childhoods lost in a decade-long blur of masks and online schooling and vaccine riots. So when this one hit, we were ready for it.

Or at least, we thought we were.

We sheltered here, with our families, and the eight of us got on fine for the first few months. We had plenty of food and water, and enough fuel to keep the generator running. But the virus didn't go away, and months turned into a year, and then another, and supplies began to run low. I've ventured out a few times, long enough to find us water, but as you know, food has been scarce. All the stores and neighboring homes have long since been looted, and wild game is scarce since the virus is killing animals just as quickly as it does people.

And then you got cancer.

We've watched it whittle you down to nothing. Your breathing sounds like the phlegmatic purring of a cat, and that's not how humans are supposed to sound. Your arms and legs are like toothpicks now. I don't know how long you have, but I'd guess maybe two or three weeks, tops. Your head looks too big for the rest of your body, and your arms and legs are like toothpicks now. You don't really have any weight left to lose. It's all gone already.

And we're not far behind.

We need to eat, brother.

So...lay back and close your eyes. I'll make sure I wait until you're asleep, and I give you my word you won't feel anything. It'll be over quick, and then you'll be at rest, and we'll be full, at least for a little while.

DELIVERY
by Brian Keene

Jorge pulls the van over to the side of the road and turns on his blinking hazard lights. Two- and three-story homes sit on wide plots of land, with well-tended yards and expensive cars in the driveways. It is a nice neighborhood. The Susquehanna River runs parallel to the road, and all of the homes have docks or boathouses on the shore. Never in a million years could Jorge afford to live here, let alone afford a boat. Maybe, if he saved up long enough, he could buy a jet ski, and then ten years after that, afford a truck and a trailer to haul it with, but actually owning a home in this part of the county? He'd have better luck getting one of those trips to Mars that Elon Musk promised he'd be handing out in another decade.

"Edna Senft," he reads aloud, doublechecking the GPS to make sure he has the correct address. Satisfied that he is indeed at the right place, Jorge slides out of the driver's seat and rummages around in the back of the van until he finds the package. It is a nondescript brown box with nothing on it to indicate what might be inside. Just his company's logo. But it is huge, easily seven feet long and when he tries to lift it, Jorge grunts with the effort.

Sighing, he dons his face mask and eyes the distance from the road to the front porch. A good twenty feet, he guesses. He could do it, but as he does at least once every day, Jorge wishes the company would provide them with dollies or carts or hand trucks—anything to help with these heavy packages. You would think, being the world's largest online retailer and one of the wealthiest companies in the world, that they would. But no, delivery contractors like Jorge are expected to provide their own. Hell, even the van is a rental.

"Yoo-hoo!"

The voice startles Jorge so much that he bangs his elbow on the van door. Wincing, he turns and sees an old white lady walking down the driveway, waving at him with one hand. Her other hand holds a gardening tool that looks like a miniature pickaxe. Her clothes are splattered with old, dried paint and fresh black soil. Gray-white hair sticks out from beneath her faded yellow AARP cap. Potting soil is smeared across her face mask, as well. He is surprised that she is wearing one. A lot of senior citizens here in Trump Country think the virus is a hoax. Jorge is also happy to see her keeping a respectful six feet distance between them.

"Can I ask you a favor, young man?"

"Sure." Jorge nods, rubbing his elbow.

"That's the gardening table I ordered."

"I don't know, ma'am. It's heavy enough to be, I guess."

"I was worried that it might be. And it's some assembly required, according to the website."

"Everything is these days."

"Yes, it sure seems to be. Although I don't mind. I was always good with tools, even before my husband died. I can put things together. I'm even better at taking them apart."

Jorge laughs. "Well, let me get this up to the porch for you, and then you can get started."

"That's the favor I was going to ask. I know your drivers usually leave packages on the front porch, but is there any chance you could carry it around back, instead?"

Inwardly, Jorge groans. But he nods his head, and says, "Sure. Not a problem. I'd be happy to."

He hefts the big box out of the van. Something metal shifts around and clangs inside.

Yes, he thinks, *that's definitely some kind of furniture.*

Grunting and straining, Jorge manages to wrestle the box up the slightly sloped driveway. Edna chatters pleasantly the entire time, talking about the weather and her plans for the table, which she says she will use to pot her many plants.

He rounds the side of the house and spies a beautiful vegetable garden and two miniature greenhouses. The rear of the house has a small attachment built on—what his grandmother used to call a mudroom. Inside this area, he sees more gardening supplies—bags of soil, along with clay pots, spray bottles and more.

Edna holds the door to the mudroom open. "If you could just put it anywhere inside, on the floor?"

Jorge hesitates. He isn't supposed to enter a customer's homes under any circumstances. Plus, there is the pandemic to think about. Carrying the package inside will put him closer than six feet to her, which increases the risk of infection. But...she is an old lady, and she's been nice. Some customers can be so rude. They are both wearing masks, and she's not coughing or sneezing or anything.

He shrugs. "Sure. I'd be happy to."

Jorge struggles, heaving the big box up over the steps and through the door. Then he drags it out of the way, over against a bare wall, and gently puts the box down. Panting, he stands up and stretches.

"There you go, m—"

Something sharp strikes him in the back of the head. The pain is incredible—white hot, almost as if he's been burned. In fact, Jorge is certain that is what has happened. Then the heat vanishes, replaced with a sudden biting cold. His vision blinks out for a moment. He tries to speak but finds that he can't. He remembers how, but his mouth doesn't seem to work. The back of his head feels sticky and wet.

He turns slowly, reaching out to keep from falling over. Edna still has the gardening tool in her hand, but he notices that now there is blood on it.

Frowning, Jorge wonders who the blood belongs to. He tries to speak again. Then he collapses.

He lies there on the floor, looking up, as Edna looms over him. As Jorge watches, she removes her mask and smiles, flashing yellow teeth that look too big for her mouth.

"I'll show you just how good I am at taking things apart." She raises the gardening tool.

Jorge tries to beg, tries to get a hand up to protect himself, but the tool slams down so fast.

The deliveryman is heavier than the gardening table she ordered, but Edna manages to get him the rest of the way into the house and down the stairs into the basement. She's nervous, and her heart is beating so fast that she seriously wonders if she's about to have a heart attack or a stroke. But her heart keeps beating, and so does Edna—giving the driver a few more good whacks just to make sure he stays unconscious until she can get him tied up.

Once he is stripped of his clothes and securely fastened to the weight bench with heavy-duty plastic zip ties and a ball gag, Edna takes a short break to catch her breath. Her doctor keeps marveling at what great shape she is in for a seventy-four-year-old, and she is. She's still able to drive and do her own shopping and putter around with her gardening every day. But this has been far more exertion than she is used to. She wishes she had done this years ago. She's been having fantasies about it since her late teens. But Harold, her late husband, would have never understood, and so, Edna had to wait him out. She's been planning since his death last year.

And she thinks she's doing great so far, if she does say so herself. She puts the driver's clothes in a garbage bag and carries it upstairs. In the gardening room, she rolls up the plastic sheeting that she'd ostensibly put down to catch both potting soil and blood. She checks the walls for blood splatter but doesn't see any. She reminds herself to check again tonight when it is dark. A few weeks ago, she ordered a kit (in fact, it was this deliveryman who brought it, although he probably doesn't remember that). The kit was made for pet owners trying to track down urine on the walls and carpet. It contains a spray bottle of Luminol and a small, pocket-sized ultraviolet flashlight.

Most nights, Edna watches the real-life crime scene investigation shows on television. Usually, she falls asleep to them.

Edna puts the plastic sheeting and the garbage bag with the clothes inside a bigger black garbage bag. She ties this closed tightly and then carries it out to the trash. Pick up is tomorrow, and she reminds herself to also make sure the trash can goes out to the curb tonight before bed.

None of her neighbors are home. It's a nice day outside, so Roger and Helaine who live in the house to the right are out on their boat. The people who live on the left, Jack and Diana, are in Florida visiting their grandchildren. Edna dons her facemask and a pair of surgical gloves, hops in to the still idling van, and drives it a mile and a half down the road to a public park. She has often seen delivery drivers parking here to have their lunch alongside the river. She pulls the van into one of the spaces and turns it off. She is not sure what to do with the keys, or with the deliveryman's wallet and phone. After debating it for a moment, she deliberately leaves the phone on the seat. She takes the keys and the wallet with her. Edna hopes that when the van is discovered, this ruse will lead investigators to think that the driver must have gone for a walk along the shore.

It takes Edna a long time to walk the mile and a half back home. When she arrives, she is even more exhausted than before. She tries to take a short nap on the couch, but she is too excited to sleep, so instead, she makes herself a cup of tea and watches some news. When the caffeine has had a chance to circulate through her system, she goes downstairs.

The driver starts moaning and whimpering as soon as he sees her. He struggles against the chains. Edna's nose wrinkles. He has made a mess all over the floor. She realizes that she forgot to put plastic down under the weight bench. Luckily, the basement has a bare concrete floor, with no carpet or tile. There's also a drain and a sump pump that Harold had installed nearly fifteen years ago, after the last big flood. She'll have to hose the basement down good when she is finished.

"I'll bring you a bucket," she says. "No more going to the bathroom on the floor or I'll make things even worse for you."

The deliveryman's eyes brim with tears. He tries begging, but the ball gag stifles his words.

"Don't," Edna advises him. "Whatever you want to say, just don't bother. I have waited a long time to do this."

She walks over to Harold's workbench. The tools have a thin layer of dust on them from disuse. Edna picks up a carpet knife and carries it back over. The driver's eyes widen. His expression is almost comical. Edna giggles.

Then she presses the blade to his scalp.

"Hold still now."

But he does not hold still. The deliveryman thrashes and bucks as much as the zip ties will allow him to. He screams beneath the gag, and thick bubbles of snot pour from his nose. Edna slices from left to right, and there is more blood than she imagined there would be. Too much blood, really. Her fingers and palm grow slick, and it is difficult to hold on to the knife. She tries to get her fingers under the wound to peel his scalp back but finds that she is unable to. She wonders if she needs to cut deeper.

Before she can try, however, the doorbell rings. Edna pauses, panicking.

The driver tenses.

She glances down at him. "I'm not expecting another delivery until Sunday. You stay put."

She puts the knife down on the floor beside him and starts up the stairs. The doorbell rings again.

"Coming!"

She hurries into the kitchen, pulse racing again, and hurriedly washes her hands. The doorbell rings a third time and then a fourth. She dries her hands and peeks out the window. Sure enough, there is another van. A man is standing on her front porch, box in hand.

Her next delivery has arrived early.

Edna goes to the door and summons her best old lady smile as she opens it.

Deacon has watched the old lady's house for a month, so he knows that she gets a lot of deliveries—at least one every few days, but sometimes multiple drop-offs in a single afternoon. It's a crazy system, and he often wonders how the world's biggest online retailer can hope to sustain it in the long term— offering free shipping, mailing it from various hubs all across the country, in multiple boxes, and having them delivered to homes by a fleet of freelancers driving both company-branded vehicles and rental vans.

Which is what he's doing. The van has been rented under an assumed name and paid for with that pseudonym's credit card.

The old lady opens the door and stares at him warily. Deacon's face is hidden by his face mask, so he tried his best to smile with his eyes. He holds up the empty box with one hand and struggles to keep his excitement and nervousness out of his voice.

"Delivery, ma'am."

"I wasn't expecting it today."

"Yeah, I know. It's the pandemic. Distribution lines are all messed up. Some stuff gets delayed for weeks. Other stuff gets shipped early. I guess it's just your lucky day."

The old lady frowns. "Well, just sit it there on the porch, if you would, please?"

"I'm afraid you have to sign for it."

Now her wary look increases. "I've never had to sign for them before."

Deacon glances up and down the road, verifies there are no witnesses, and then shoves the box through the small opening in the door. The old lady takes an instinctive step backward, releasing her hold on the door. He shoves it open quickly and then slams it shut behind him. Before she can react, he yanks the gun from beneath his shirt and points it at her. The old lady's eyes widen.

"Easy now," he says. "Don't make me use this. Just relax."

"I...what...what do you want? I don't keep any cash here."

"I'm not going to hurt you," he lies. "Just do what I say, and you won't get hurt. Understand?"

Swallowing, she slowly nods. Her eyes blink rapidly. Her hands flutter and flex.

Too late, Deacon realizes that he left his bag with all the tools and the ropes and handcuffs inside the van. His plan was to do it in her bedroom, but without his equipment, there will be no way to tie her up. And if he can't tie her up, it won't be as exciting.

"Do you have a basement?"

She nods again. There's something in her expression—something he can't define.

Deacon waggles the gun. "Show me. And don't fuck around, lady. You try anything, and I'll fucking kill you."

She leads him down a hallway toward the back of the house. She stops at a door just beyond the kitchen. Past the door, he glimpses a laundry room or something. It's full of gardening stuff. She points at the door with one trembling finger.

"Here. It's down here."

He motions with the gun again. "Ladies first."

The door creaks as the old lady opens it. She starts down a flight of similarly creaky wooden stairs, and he follows along. Deacon sniffs and then scowls. It smells like shit and piss down here. The old lady reaches the bottom before him and moves off to one side.

"Hey! Stay where you fucking are. I didn't—"

Deacon pauses at the bottom, gaping. There is a naked man with a ball gag stuffed in his mouth and tied to a weight bench. His face is slathered in blood, and there's a large, wet cut around the base of his scalp.

Deacon stares at the man. "What the fuck?"

He turns toward the old lady just in time to see her swinging some kind of gardening tool, the end of which buries itself in his left eye. Shrieking, Deacon stumbles backward. The old lady curses and grunts, sounding more like a wild animal than a human being. She wrenches the tool free, widening his eye socket in the process. She raises it for another blow and—with his one remaining eye—Deacon sees bits of himself clinging to the weapon. He raises the gun and as the tool strikes him again, he fires a single shot directly into the elderly woman's abdomen. The impact knocks her backward onto the stairs. Deacon hears something snap. The old lady wails. Her cries are the last thing he hears. He slumps to the floor. Something is very wrong with his head, but he's not sure what. He drops the gun and gently feels his forehead with his fingers, probing. He stops when he finds a wide hole.

Then he dies.

Edna dies forty-seven minutes later from blood loss and shock. She is grateful as she feels herself lose consciousness, because it means a release from the agony of the hip she broke when she fell.

Jorge watches as the last bit of steam rises from their cooling bodies in the cold basement. Then he is alone. He struggles against his restraints but has no luck. Worse, the effort makes his nose runny, which in turn makes it hard to breathe. He focuses instead on the ball gag. Not only does it make breathing more difficult, but his jaw is beginning to ache. Between that, the cramps in his legs, and the steady, rhythmic throb in his injured head, it is hard to focus, and soon, Jorge stops pushing against the ball gag with his tongue. It's not going to come loose, and it's better to save his strength.

Sooner or later, someone will figure out he's missing. The van had a GPS tracker. And even if they don't, the old lady told him she was expecting another delivery. He can't remember when she said it was supposed to come. But eventually, another driver will show up.

They *have* to.

Crying, Jorge waits for someone to deliver him.

A CONVERSATION WITH BRIAN KEENE
by Gabino Iglesias

In 2011, the World Horror Convention was held in Austin, TX. I was there, talking to people and interviewing horror authors for two different venues I was writing for at the time. Brian Keene was there. I was a fan of his work, but I didn't interview him because some folks had told me he was an asshole.

In November of 2012, I was in Portland, OR for BizarroCon. My first book came out that weekend and I was excited and scared because I knew how much I ignored, and nothing is as scary as truly understanding the depth of your ignorance. Keene was there as well. This time, things were different. I ran into him outside an event and said "Mr. Keene, I'm Gabino. Huge fan of your work. I was in Austin last year. I didn't talk to you because folks had told me you were an asshole." He laughed. We sat down in the hallway. He told me how things work. He explained how we opt to be public figures, but our families don't and thus should be protected. He told me about paying it forward. I listened. I took notes. I applied everything he said to my career.

Now it's 2022 and I'm interviewing a man I consider a mentor, a brother, and an inspiration. And I'm not alone on this: several generations of writers consider Keene not only an influence but also a sort or rock-and-roll father figure to the genre. It's great to see him get this honor. Here's a little conversation we had using this as an excuse.

GABINO IGLESIAS (GI): You've been doing this thing for more than two decades (you know, despite still being a young cat!). You've seen presses, fads, and writers come and go, and you're still here. This isn't an easy business. What keeps you going?

BRIAN KEENE (BK): A few things, I think, but one in particular. I was a fan of the horror genre—be it books, movies, or comics—long before I ever became a professional. And after all these years, I'm still a fan. You're right that this isn't an easy business, but I still love coming to work each day, because I love what I do. I have the opportunity to give back to a genre that has given me so much enjoyment and comfort and entertainment over the years. That's a pretty awesome thing. And it's a repeatable thing. It was cool when my fellow Gen X'ers were reading my books. It was cool all over again a decade later when Millennials discovered my books from their parents or their older brothers and sisters. And it's really cool now as Zoomers are discovering my stuff for the first time. That's three generations of horror fans I've been able to entertain and to—hopefully—expand their awareness of everything this genre has to offer.

Another factor is that I'm too fucking old now to do anything else. Seriously. I'm fifty-four now, and I've done all the other jobs. I did them all before writing full-time. If I quit writing today and went back to the foundry or the loading docks or driving truck or roofing, I'd be dead inside a year. Those are not easy jobs. Writing isn't an easy job either, but it's way less physically taxing than factory work or manual labor. I've got a Navy buddy. Same age as me. He works construction. He loves his job, but he also acknowledges the toll it is taking on his body after all this time. Writing takes its toll, too, but I'll take carpal tunnel over what he's dealing with any day of the week.

GI: You gave me some words of advice back in 2012 that I still live by and have added to that with words and actions many times since. To many in my generation, you're more than a role model; you're a mentor. You're always teaching others to pay it forward, and we do. Who helped you out and taught you to use one hand to climb up and one to help those coming up behind you?

BK: Lists like this are dangerous, because every time I've done one over the years, I have inevitably, unintentionally left somebody out, and then I feel terrible. So, to try to avoid that, I'm just going to list the people who helped me in a very big way. All of whom, incidentally, also used one hand to climb and the other hand to pull folks from my generation up. Richard Laymon and John Pelan both read my first novel and about a dozen of my earliest short stories and gave me lots of feedback. And Laymon wrote an introduction to my first collection and introduced me to the editor of that first novel. Jack Ketchum taught me how to negotiate the contract for that first novel, and then gave me even more feedback on the novel itself. Over the years, F. Paul Wilson, Joe R. Lansdale, and David J. Schow have been there any time I needed advice or (occasionally) a swift kick in the ass. Mary is fond of saying "Nobody can make Brian do something he doesn't want to do—except Paul, Joe or David." And she's right. The three of them have always steered me right.

And later on in my career, Stephen King, who gave me some unexpected and unsolicited kind words at one of the absolute darkest moments of my life—at a time when I was seriously going to quit and go back to one of those other jobs we talked about earlier. He didn't know I needed that, but he did it anyway, out of sheer kindness. Also, later in my career—something that I don't think anyone other than Mary knows about. When the World Horror Convention gave me the Grandmaster Award, the organizers for that year refused to pay for my travel, and—that was shortly after horror had imploded and was on one of those down swings, so I couldn't afford the airfare. John Skipp and Tim Waggoneer paid for it, instead. Had it not been for them, I wouldn't have been there to accept my award.

As someone who was a fan of these guys long before I ever met any of them, I still trip over the help, assistance, and—in many cases—friendship that they've offered over the years. Simple little acts of kindness that, on the surface, probably don't seem like much. But each of them knew how much it meant—and means. And I know how much it means when I do it for someone new. I know that, even now, if I'm having some crisis of the soul, I can call Joe or David (depending on the time—Joe's a morning person like me, and David keeps a vampire's hours) and they can talk me off the ledge, or point me in the right direction, or tell me I'm being an asshole. And you,

Gabino, know that you can call me and get the same. And I see you starting to do it for folks coming up behind you. And that's a beautiful thing, and it makes this often infuriating profession a little bit better.

GI: As someone who has seen so much, where do you think horror fiction stands right now?

BK: If you study the history of publishing and horror fiction (including the time periods when Horror didn't exist as a marketing label)—it runs in cycles. There are seven to ten year stretches where horror fiction is red hot in popularity and sales. Then there are five to seven year stretches when it wanes in popularity. Right now, we are in the middle of an upswing, and it's hotter than it's ever been. Eventually, things will cool off again.

But there's one big difference now. The mid-list doesn't exist at the bookstore anymore. Instead, it has moved online and is fostered by the indie presses. And given the significant growth of indie publishing, and the tools and technology available to not only publishers, but to authors, as well—even during the next downturn, when horror once again disappears from the bookstore shelves, readers will still be able to find it in abundance. The only real danger in that is an oversaturation of the market—when there is more horror fiction being published than there are consumers who are interested in it. And that will happen, too. But then another upswing will come about. It's all cyclical.

GI: From self-publishing to ebooks, horror has changed a lot. What's the most significant change you've experienced and how has it impacted your career?

BK: I think it's what I just said—the rise of independent publishing. Look at what companies like Valancourt are doing. Thanks to the technology and the distribution system, they are able to present long-lost seminal works of horror fiction to a new generation of readers—books that should have never gone out of print, but did. Or look at presses like Grindhouse. Not only do they provide a home and a decent income to authors like Bryan Smith, who was really impacted by the loss of the mid-list, but they can also spotlight the next generation. Novels like Samantha Kolesnik's *True Crime*, which I don't think any mainstream publisher would have taken a chance on, but Grindhouse was able to get it out there to the public, and now everyone is talking about that book. Or Crossroads Press, who are providing a home for so many older authors, all of whom are still writing and still have stories to tell, but many of whom seem to have been forgotten by mainstream publishing.

And I think that last thing is really important. I started in this business in 1997, and we—as an industry and as a community—have made clear, demonstrable strides when it comes to representation and marginalized communities. Can we still do better? Of course. But there's a big difference between then and now. But I feel strongly that ageism is still a factor in this industry, and it's not something that gets talked about a lot. We need to have that discussion. And I'm not just saying that because I'm now in my early fifties (laughs). I'm saying that because I see the struggles of authors twenty years my senior. Authors whom I grew up reading. And those struggles are very real. So, it's good that there are safe places for them to go. But I think we need to do more.

GI: We're doing this interview because you're a Guest of Honor this year. What does this mean to you?

BK: It's an honor. People might not know this, but long before I ever sold a book, one of the first gigs I had in this business was as Associate Editor for the HWA Newsletter. I've got long-time, deep ties to the organization. We haven't always gotten along, but that's only because I always wanted this organization to be the best it could be. We need it. Desperately. And there were years when I felt it was not serving us, and I was vocal about that. But I think most folks understand where I was coming from in those times. If you disagree with the people in charge—be they your government or your bosses or the heads of your writing organization—you speak up. And now, of course, we've got a great team steering the ship. It's like a new Golden Age for the HWA. I'm tickled to be here. I know you're listing me as a Guest of Honor, but truly, the honor is mine. I'm humbled.

GI: You have a unique perspective when it comes to publishing. You have published your own work, worked with great independent presses, and published with Big Four. I think all writers could benefit from some pointers. What matters when it comes to publishing? What do you look for when deciding how to treat a project?

BK: It all depends on the project itself. Some books, like *Pressure* or *Castaways*, have mainstream appeal, so I sold them to mainstream publishers. Others, like *The Girl on the Glider* or *The Complex*, were either too weird or too over the top to ever have mainstream appeal, so I sold those to indie presses. And some, like my non-fiction collections, for example, have an admittedly limited appeal, so I choose to self-publish those.

There are also other things to consider. I think novellas are the perfect length for horror fiction, but it's incredibly hard to sell a novella-length work to one of the Big Four. So, for something like that, I usually send it to an indie publisher. But something that's 100,000 words long and not insane, I'll try the Big Four with it. And then there are oddball works that you have to think about carefully. *End of the Road*, for example. I knew that book would do well with libraries, and with horror fiction fans. But I also knew that none of the Big Four wanted 'Brian Keene's book-length non-fiction musings on the history of modern horror fiction and how to (poorly) come to terms with grief and loss.' So, Cemetery Dance was the perfect fit for that. Libraries could easily order from them. So could horror fiction fans. And editors Rich Chizmar and Blu Gilliand didn't try to ride herd over me or control the message the way a Big Four editor would have been required to do. The mainstream publishing marketing departments would have balked the moment I wrote about planning to steal my best friend's remains from where he was interred. But Rich and Blu were like, "Just don't get caught." (laughs)

GI: Every legend from Stephen King to Joe Lansdale has something to say about the role of reading in a writer's life. I want your thoughts because you're always reading and talk about what you're reading in your newsletter. How much do you read these days? How do you make the time for it while juggling various projects and deadlines?

BK: My answer is going to make the HWA and StokerCon® officials regret their decision to have me as a Guest of Honor, but—I read on the toilet. Seriously. The toilet and the bathtub. Here's my average day: Get up at 5am. Take my pills and exercise. Start writing at 6am. Around 8am, nature calls and I sit on the toilet and read for twenty minutes. I could be out of there in five minutes, because I'm pretty regular, but I get distracted by whatever I'm reading and don't really notice until my legs have gone to sleep.

I write until about 2pm every day. Then I either take an hour's nap (in the winter) or go for a hike (when the weather is nice). Around 3pm, I run a hot bubble bath, and I soak until about 4pm or 4:30. And that's when I get most of my reading time. Those sixty or ninety minutes. Then, around 4:30 I make dinner for Mary and I. Then we spend the evening together. Or, if she has to write that night, I might go back to work a little, or play X-Box, or read some more.

So yeah. The toilet and the tub. Aren't you glad you asked?

GI: Readers of your work come in many forms, but those who have been reading you for a while know of the Keene Mythos. How did that come about? When did you decide to have recurring themes, places, and characters in your oeuvre?

BK: It was there from the very start. The first two comic books I ever read were *The Defenders* #33 and *Captain America and The Falcon* #196. Both were published by Marvel Comics, and though this was my first introduction to their characters, I was immediately struck by the fact that these two seemingly independent books were actually linked to each other. They took place in a shared universe and referenced other characters and occurrences—not just from previous issues of their own individual series, but from other comic books also published by the company. Understand, the year was 1975, and this type of thing was unheard of at the time. Sure, H.P. Lovecraft's mythos took place in a shared continuity, but Lovecraft's stuff was impossible to find in rural Pennsylvania in 1975, and even if I'd had access to it, I probably wouldn't have been allowed to read it at such an early age. Soon after, I discovered DC Comics, and another shared universe! And after that, I was not only buying new issues from both publishers—I was also riding my bike to the flea market and yard sales on the weekend, snapping up any back issues I could find and valiantly trying to piece together the larger, uber-narrative of the shared universe itself.

A few years later, when then-new horror authors like Stephen King and F. Paul Wilson began dropping hints throughout their various works that their books and stories were also taking place in shared universes, I remember the adults around me expressing surprise at this. To them, this was something new and bold, but to me, I thought it was what writers were supposed to do.

So, it was my explicit intention from Day One that everything I wrote—be it a short story, a novella, a novel, or a comic book—would be set in the same universe. A shared universe, just like those I'd grown up reading. I began writing for publication around 1993. I sold my first story in 1997. I sold my first novel in 2002. All of them were connected in my head.

GI: Now tell me about Brian Keene and his life impacting Brian Keene's work. I'm thinking not only about all your nonfiction/biographical stuff but also "fiction" like *The Girl on the Glider*. How much reality seeps into your fiction? Do you allow it and embrace it or try to keep it under control?

BK: I mean…(long pause)…we all do it, to some extent, whether we want to admit to it or not. But there have been times where I went too far with it, and I have deep regrets about those times. Chapter Two of *Dark Hollow*, for example. I am very close with my ex-wife, Cassandra. Indeed, she remains one of my best friends, and she and Mary are close, as well. But that chapter… see, we'd miscarried not once, but three times. And

I was a lot younger and a lot stupider then, and while I listened to her when she talked about how it made her feel, I didn't communicate my feelings to her. Instead, I wrote about them. And what I wrote was pretty goddamned raw. And it hurt her—me putting that out into the world, instead of sharing it with her first. I'll always regret that. I mean, she's forgiven me, and like I said, we're best friends, but I'll still carry that guilt with me probably until I die.

I didn't know my father was reading my books until *Ghoul* came out in paperback. He called me one night, at like one in the morning. I thought someone must have died, because it was so late. And my dad was crying, and when I asked him what was wrong, he said, "I'm sorry for ripping up your comic books when you were a kid." Because I'd used that for a scene in the book.

So, yeah...there have been times I wish I hadn't. But the flip side of that is that there have been books and stories that wouldn't have resonated as much as they did, if I hadn't done that. You mentioned *The Girl on the Glider*, and that's obvious. But there's less obvious stuff. That scene in *The Complex* when the main character is considering selling his Bram Stoker Awards® because he's broke? That was me at one point. Or that chapter in *Clickers vs. Zombies* about making peace with divorce? J.F. Gonzalez once told me he thought it was one of the most beautiful, honest things I ever wrote, and nobody would notice it because I hid it inside a pulp horror novel about demonically-possessed corpses fighting giant crab monsters. And he was right.

But we all do it. My dear friend Tom Piccirilli lost his father when he was very young. Just about everything Pic ever wrote has some element of that in it. It haunted him his whole life, and it's there, in his fiction. Sometimes it was subtle, and other times it overflowed.

GI: I know this is the question all writers hate, but I think it's special because of the context of this interview. What's next for you? Sure, tell me about upcoming projects, but what also the long run. Where do you see yourself in half a decade? You play the grouchy old man well, but you still have decades of words in you...

BK: For the first time in my career, I have no deadlines. And I won't lie—it's both invigorating and a little unnerving. I'm at a point where I can write whatever I want to write, and there's an indescribable feeling of creative freedom that comes with that. But there's also some uncertainty. What if I spend four months working on something, and nobody wants to read it? And I worry about this *Labyrinth* series, which is supposed to wrap up my mythos nice and neat with a pretty little bow and bring everything to an end. The first two books are written and published. I'm in the midst of writing the third book now. There are three more to follow after that. I have this fear deep inside of, "What if I don't get these finished?" I'd hate to do that to my readers. So, even though I don't have any publisher deadlines, I have an internal deadline when it comes to those.

But for whatever time remains, I'll just keep writing, so not much will change. I could slow down now, if I wanted to, but the workhorse in me still sticks to the schedule. Six in the morning until two in the afternoon. Butt in chair. Fingers on keyboard. That is the way things get written. Maybe there are other methods, but this is the only way I know. You can still teach this old dog some new tricks, if you have any to share, but this has always been the method that works for me.

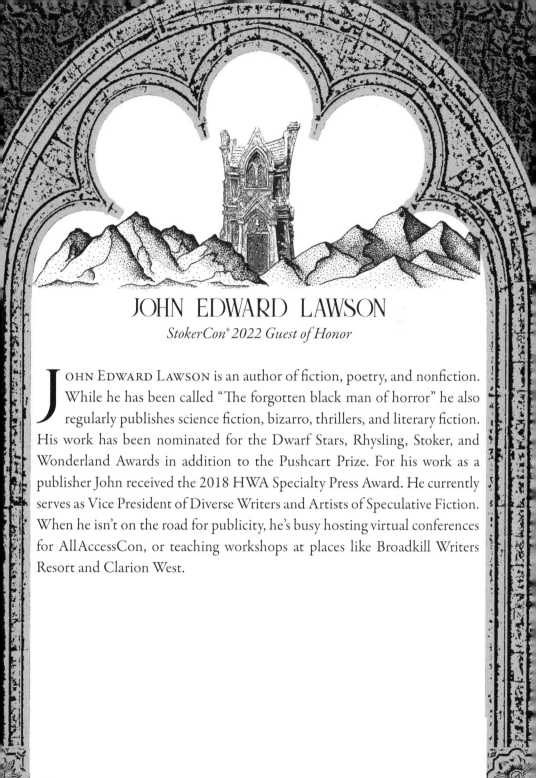

JOHN EDWARD LAWSON
StokerCon® 2022 Guest of Honor

JOHN EDWARD LAWSON is an author of fiction, poetry, and nonfiction. While he has been called "The forgotten black man of horror" he also regularly publishes science fiction, bizarro, thrillers, and literary fiction. His work has been nominated for the Dwarf Stars, Rhysling, Stoker, and Wonderland Awards in addition to the Pushcart Prize. For his work as a publisher John received the 2018 HWA Specialty Press Award. He currently serves as Vice President of Diverse Writers and Artists of Speculative Fiction. When he isn't on the road for publicity, he's busy hosting virtual conferences for AllAccessCon, or teaching workshops at places like Broadkill Writers Resort and Clarion West.

YEARS OF DECAY

by John Edward Lawson

1

Daniel David studies the ink rippling under his skin as it surges in time with his muscles, while someone's fingernails carve new wounds across his old scars. A relief map of reknit tissue along his arm is nearly as faded as the tattoos telling his life story. Those tattoos would be more extensive, have more to say, save for the fact his life already ended, cut short so long ago.

Almost as short as that of the man struggling in his grasp. His black clothes looked to be roughly Daniel David's size, and weather-resistant as well. They will serve as excellent replacements for the current ensemble of stained, tattered rags bound to his skin by rope. The Heckler & Koch 416D, semi-automatic Benelli M4, and Beretta 92F 9-millimeter had run out of ammo, then came apart after being repurposed as tools over the years. The tactical vest eventually had to be cast aside because it was punctured scores of times over. The ballistic helmet was hopelessly fractured, and the Taser X26 ran out of juice years before the Motorola radio finally stopped transmitting. The last of his equipment to survive were canisters full of flex cuffs, thankfully not so biodegradable as tree-huggers would have wanted way back in the day.

Now that he stopped to consider it: why should Daniel David desire the other man's clothes? Seasons had ceased to change so long ago that he cannot accurately recall the passage of time. Besides, extremes of heat and cold no longer hold any power over his resolve.

It does not matter that the man's bladder begins to empty into his trousers as the radius of Daniel David's right forearm refuses to snap against his windpipe. Pungent odors will not deter Daniel David from donning the garb. The sensations which have filled the void since Carrie left would break the sanity of lesser men, so he shuts them out.

A steel knife suddenly occupies space in Daniel David's left thigh. The metal penetrates several inches of rectus femoris and sartorius before the tip directly explores his femur. The stranger miscalculated if he thought this pain would improve his fate. The musculature of Daniel David's face contracts as the result of some involuntary muscle memory, with the corners of his mouth turning upwards while his lips part to expose his teeth.

Carrie had enjoyed this aspect of his appearance, telling him it was charming.

At the thought of her voice—and its lack of malice or terror or duplicity—Daniel David snaps the man's neck.

Why? Because.

2

Collapsed buildings lean together forming a pyramid, their empty windows giving voice to the wind's laments. The steel and concrete had twisted into this architectural chimera after a series of blasts set by demonstrators, protesters, Occupiers and leftists, and Libertarians and white supremacists. Nobody held a monopoly on violent paranoia after the epidemic grew out of control. Crowning this brick-and-mortar monument to failure is the flame. That fire has kept Daniel David anchored to this spot. If he fails to keep the fire going, Carrie will not know where to find him, will think that he died or that he was too weak-willed to cut it in her absence.

He prefers to remember Carrie as she was on that one perfect day when they were at Sheriff Mahfouz's home for an evening of toasts and presentations and more variety of food than Daniel David could hope to sample. The head of the State Sheriff's Association himself snapped a picture of Carrie embracing Daniel David in the dappled shade of a magnolia in the estate's large backyard. They both had unabashed smiles which revealed how utterly smitten they were with each other and with what they perceived as their shared future.

Then the future arrived in the form of multiple extinction level events. Social effects of the final war had been somewhat mitigated, and there were stopgap measures for the disease, but the environmental deviations were enough to force the bulk of survivors underground. However, none of the spaceships hastily built by the elite had been launched due to startup sequence errors. That was the rumor, anyway.

Daniel David is one of the few hundred original squatters to claim the collapsed network of structures now forming the pyramid. That population rapidly dwindled, until the only company he now keeps is that of loners who come after hearing tell of a purifying fire at the pyramid's zenith. It is said the fire—by means of the machinery attached to it—burns away the disease. They were violent, desperate scavengers. Where had they come from? Nobody would ever know. These loners are secrets to be interred in the conspiracy database out back alongside thousands of co-conspirators under loose soil.

It is the intersection of roads at the pyramid's base that makes the pilgrimage possible for survivors of the blasted landscape, and the shadowy things now inhabiting it. Only one or two of these unknown and unknowable personalities find their way to him per week. The interim between such visits are what Daniel David terms "lean times."

Why? Because evil.

3

One day, specialists had ridden in on a machine unlike any Daniel David had ever seen before. Nobody knew what to expect: was this some remnant of a military convoy? Where could they possibly be going?

"To end this, of course."

As an answer, that sounded simple enough. How could Carrie not go for that? Ending it. Weaklings always found the struggle too much to bear, and could not endure the day in, day out of it. Supposedly, the population of specialists housed in the enormous and elaborate vehicle could physics themselves in and out of all sorts of different dimensional coordinates.

A knee injury had ended Daniel David's MMA career in his youth, but that did not mean he was not still a man, one honorable and capable of bringing the fuck-you-up attitude when need be. Everyone began looking at him sideways, though, when he was not gung-ho about jumping in some stranger's contraption to abandon the home they had built, to essentially gut the community. The bulk of his clan was going along with the scientists in their crazy scheme to find a cure for the disease, to try and reverse the permanent darkness blanketing the Earth, and who knew what else.

Since then how many mothers has he witnessed put to death, how many children beheaded or devoured alive, how many grown men reduced to their component parts as they watch, unable to halt their own slow-motion demise?

Carrie would make sense of it all. Just seeing her again. There is nothing carnal about this notion; his tenements of lust were condemned ages ago, deserted for the promise of standing in her presence just one more time with the flashblindness caused by looking directly at her, and the overpressure of her voice rolling over him in waves. It would be enough to sit next to her in comfortable silence as the machines processed their blood, straining out new variants of the virus.

But the brainiacs had insisted on taking her away. They had even slung some incendiary rubbish about dragging him along with them. But somebody had to stay behind to act as a shepherd to maintain the medical distribution systems just in case they came back with the cure they sought. He was the man for that job, he insisted, because he could endure it.

Carrie had not been able to meet his eyes at that moment, nor did she say goodbye.

When the interlopers stab him, burn him, or bludgeon his bones with lengths of metal they always look right at him. That brief human connection is what keeps him going. And the scientists, the doctors, and specialists, they had said he wouldn't make it. That he would change over time.

Why? Because evil...

4

The fire was originally meant as a beacon, a rallying point, not an actual cure, but over time, perception can alter reality. As more and more survivors arrived and were disposed of, Daniel David came to perceive himself as the cure. The cure for human weakness.

The subject of weakness—more to the point, how it influenced the desire for change—was always one of hot debate between himself and Carrie. She was always on the move, upwardly mobile and ambitious, for which he criticized her as being stuck in a hamster ball, convinced a change of scenery meant she did not have to improve herself. For her part she accused him of externalizing his own problems and seeing them everywhere he looked, causing him to live in fear of change.

The experts told Daniel David that if he stayed, he would be gradually altered, that he would eventually succumb, but they were just afraid of seeing him strong enough to survive on his own. He found that remaining in the resting place of their relationship caused his strength to grow exponentially.

The machinery was not responsible for altering his condition. His genes and willpower drove him onward. He kept the machines in top form, just in case. Just in case those crazy bastards did somehow make it back to the right time and place instead of getting stuck somewhere hundreds of thousands of years before the Ice Age trying to retrieve some extinct plant. He would do his duty and maintain the equipment just as he maintained his own physique. After all, the survivors continued to trickle in, all of them baring weapons and hatred and inexplicable greed for the fire.

Or, perhaps not so inexplicable considering Daniel David's penchant for suggesting by means of radio there might, in fact, be a cure awaiting any who made it to the pyramid's fiery pinnacle. He perpetrated these broadcasts back when he actually preserved some hope Carrie's mission might succeed, and that her team would phase back into the timeline without a hiccup. Those messages were meant to build a new community with which to impress Carrie on her return. He ended those transmissions soon enough, but the damage had already been done.

And the ceaseless stream of interlopers continues to trickle in.

Why? Because evil...never...

5

The silence is broken by someone unfamiliar with the terrain attempting to surmount the pyramid. There are at least three of them. Feet slip and dislodge bits of crumbling wall.

"Why do you even wanna see this place?"

"Yeah, is it because of the legend?"

Those two voices belong to men, but the third member of their expedition remains silent. Daniel David does not bother moving from his perch. He has been motionless for the better part of a day. Or two. Or three. The thin layer of grime coating his skin suggests a sizable lean time has passed since he last troubled himself with anything. A brief test of his joints reveals he has not lost his prowess.

"She doesn't know about the legend."

"Lookit. See there? Nobody ever gets up to that fire and comes back down."

"Sure, some folks make it up there. They been seen up there. Why they never get seen again is anybody's guess."

"A certain contingent always say it cured them, so why they wanna come back? Course they don't. Them's the hopeful ones. Most folks don't believe in that foolishness. We know the real reason."

"See, there's a vampire what lives up in these here ruins."

Silence, followed by trudging, grunts, and a snicker.

"She don't believe us."

"I wouldn't either!"

"Smell that?" The group pauses, hesitates, lurks in the same spot a moment too long. "Your nose don't lie. We all done smelled death in our time, but that there smell ain't natural. It's worse than death."

Supernatural cures, supernatural curses, it is always the same with humanity's last few remnants. Daniel David and his message are irrelevant in the final equation. The deceit others experience is not due to his words so much as their own incessant desire to believe in something greater, tales of Heaven and divine reward. Primitive intelligence is what doomed them. They are beholden to what Daniel David refers to as Bronze Age modes of reasoning.

The group continues moving, but not before Daniel David has descended in a single fluid motion to explore the weakness of the rear man's soft flesh.

Soon enough, these three will be drained of their vital fluids. The machine designed to filter the virus out long ago depleted the supply of raw materials, necessitating these harvests. The weak perish so the strong might live.

Children only contain about 1.75 liters of blood which, in addition to their constant neediness and uncultured nature, renders them next to useless. They serve well enough to keep the lean times at bay, though.

The lead pair continue for half a minute before realizing something is remiss. They shift in the darkness, calling out for their companion. Before they know what is happening the remaining man has compound fractures of the ulna and fibula, with crushed ribs on the way.

The woman turns away and runs. She is within ten yards of the fire, and the machines surrounding it, when Daniel David's hand finds her shoulder blade. She tumbles through the air, screaming on her descent, but not for long. He follows her down the pyramid's other side.

She is impaled on a strand of rebar still embedded in the pyramid's concrete. The exposed end has been meticulously sharpened for just such an opportunity, as has all the pyramid's other bits of protruding metal. The face staring up at Daniel David in wonder and bewilderment is Carrie's.

That is impossible, yet the voice squeaking out broken syllables also matches his memory of her. She is begging him for help, begging him to respond. What can he possibly say to her? Something to ease her passing, or perhaps something to make it all the more excruciating? She is the one, after all, who had forsaken him on this useless mound, left him overseer of the diseased and the dead, chronicler of unending darkness. To what gain? In the end, her choices cannot have possibly been worth it.

"Th-the cure...we found it...I'm the last one, baby, but I never gave up... knew I'd...I'd see you again. Here," she says, gesturing to a satchel at her side. "Inside. Take it. Put it...put it in the machine. Activate...activate the aerosol dispersal sequence and...and...and the human race can rebound. Rebuild."

Words finally fail her, so she instead smiles up at him and, for once, he can admit she is the first person to do so in what for him is several hundred years, but likely much less for her—possibly even just weeks or days in time travels. At her continued urging, he withdraws a tube full of luminescent blue liquid, framed by some unfamiliar metal alloy. After a cursory examination, he figures out the locking mechanism and undoes it, tossing the metal away so that he might hold the tube up to firelight for scrutiny.

In his gut, something is horribly awry. There is pain, or...fear? Yes! The sensation is so unfamiliar as to be simultaneously thrilling and enough to cut his legs out from under him. Muscles contract, curling him into a ball, and his paralyzed hand is unable to relinquish its grip on the tube. This thing and its contents spell the end for him. All his power siphoned away with the push of a button.

Daniel David looks from the cure to the beatific agony of the woman he loves, and for a moment he views exactly how to save her, how to relieve her impalement and nurse her back to health. Then the strength which has been nurtured in Carrie's absence wakes and, roused to action, plunges the glass tube into her oral cavity. Blue liquid and shattered teeth spray everywhere, and Carrie's scream fails to compete with the sound of glass splintering in her tonsils and esophagus.

Daniel David thrusts his violence into her repeatedly until she is riddled with bloody wounds, and yet somehow she is unable to succumb in the same fashion as others would. Perhaps she had been on to something all along, and change really is inevitable; apparently one undergoes certain refinements and alterations regardless of whether they stay with the smell of smoke and charred wood or instead go skipping all around time and space. It seems she will have limitless occasions to enjoy being right as he continues to measure her capacity for pain against the scope of his willpower.

Will Jared have evolved in the same manner as Daniel David and Carrie? Jared had spent years with Daniel David, far longer than Carrie had, functioning as a proxy brother. Daniel David had not grown up with siblings, so he took such close friendships seriously. Then the quest to find an uncorrupted water source had been proposed, resulting in Jared being the first to volunteer and abandon Daniel David via that suicide mission.

Contemplating this betrayal is beyond angering.

Jared had, in the end, been unable to stand the burden of daily survival as a proper adult should, had been a lesser man whose word meant little in the final analysis, and despite this—or, perhaps because of it—Daniel David must stay vigilant over the flame to ensure it remains as his friend remembered it.

Just in case...just in case...just in case.

He has to tend the fire...

Because evil never dies.

A CONVERSATION WITH JOHN EDWARD LAWSON

by Michele Brittany and Nicholas Diak

John Lawson is a modern-day renaissance man: poet, writer, publisher, musician, businessman, and even a conference and writers retreat organizer via the AllAccessCon and Broadkill Resort endeavors. He has been an invaluable pillar of the horror writer's community through his contributions, his creative output and his lifting, promoting, and motivating of other writers. His various accolades are a testament to his accomplishments: he was nominated for a Bram Stoker Award for Poetry Collection in 2006 for the *Troublesome Amputee,* he and Jennifer Barnes received the 2018 Specialty Press Award for Raw Dog Screaming Press, and in 2022 he is one of the guests of honor for StokerCon®.

We are honored to have interviewed John via email for this book to underscore his contributions to the horror community.

NICHOLAS AND MICHELE (N&M): John, you and your wife Jennifer Barnes are the founders of the Raw Dog Screaming Press (RDSP) and you both received the Specialty Press Award from the Horror Writers Association in 2018. What did that recognition from the horror community mean for you both? What makes RDSP unique from other indie publishers?

JOHN EDWARD LAWSON (JEL): Raw Dog Screaming Press has been in operation twenty years now, and our success was never a certainty. In fact, due to our focus on cross-genres books that other publishers won't sign because they're more difficult to market, some people were skeptical or even downright hostile toward us for a while. To know the horror community recognizes our efforts, and the work of our amazing authors, it's still a bit mind-blowing, to be honest. More importantly, as we view it, that recognition confirms we are on the right track. We intend to double and triple down on publishing horror, and helping authors build careers rather than dumping them if they don't hit X number of sales in their first four weeks.

Our mode of operation has always been one focused on the long term. We strive to build with purpose, to build toward something rather than just chase dollars. There will always be more dollars because there's a whole industry with factories making them, and for authors who could thrive in the "Big Four" high-sales-goal environment we try to pass on those projects and direct them to the proper editors at other houses. If you've been in the publishing scene long enough you begin to notice a pattern of new publishers trying to go big in the short term, who make a splash and then flame out within two or three years, never to be heard from again.

Having a team running the company has made all the difference for preventing that from happening. The struggle is real, but we're able to share duties and keep burnout at bay for the most part, or see creative opportunities, or play to our individual strengths as marketers or designers or editors. We were also among the first wave of hybrid publishers using print on demand as a printing and distribution model, not as some vanity press scheme, giving indie writers a chance at traditional publishing. Another piece of that is we, unlike a lot of publishers I guess, are very serious about negotiating with authors and trying to make the contract work for them. Or, just as important, allowing more room for creative freedom and support of the release long after it is no longer "new" —because if somebody hasn't read it yet, the book is still new to them.

A lot of excellent publishers are in the HWA community, with each specializing in their own flavor of horror. We just hope to live up to their standards while we continue exploring offbeat and unexpected manuscripts.

N&M: What is the most useful advice you received as a writer/publisher, and what advice can you give to writers?

JEL: During my first couple years attending industry conferences, there were two established veterans who imparted crucial advice without even realizing they were doing so. Michael A. Arnzen, at that point a winner of the Stoker Award and the International Horror Guild Award in addition to being a professor and published all over, said at my first World Horror Convention (Kansas City, 2003) that he didn't get into hierarchical thinking. This was in response to my suggestion that, while finally meeting in person after our online correspondence was cool, there were probably other people he should be networking with besides a newbie like me. From that point forward I've taken the position of not being into hierarchical thinking either, and I feel this approach is one of the secret weapons driving our success as a publishing company. Publishers and editors should be business partners with writers, from new to established authors, not wielding power over them.

Bumping into Thomas F. Monteleone at the Stoker Awards in New York City, 2004, was fortunate because one of the many things he imparted to Jennifer and me was that, as publishers just starting out we needed to understand the importance of always having another book in the process of being published. The advice may seem strange or even daunting, but later, as I studied business—yes, taking business classes after launching a company is a bit like closing the barn door after the horses have already eaten your children—one of the things I learned about was called the economy of scale. The more you're printing the cheaper the cost, the more titles you publicize with each appearance or ad the less the publicity costs per book, and so forth. The advice also applies to writing, acting, podcasting, music, you name it.

The next advice is a combination of things I was told fused with things picked up from experience. Whenever I speak on publishing careers, I always mention that it's a battle of attrition. Don't give up. It's tough not to! But if you stick around, in a couple years you're taken seriously, and in five to ten years you're one of the people to watch. That's due to the aforementioned flame-out syndrome. Making it to that place is easier when you remember the chances you get are the ones you make, which I suppose has been conveyed more recently by language about the hustle and the grind. However, you prefer to think of it, taking advantage of those opportunities often requires you to have skills outside your job description, or be willing to think outside the box. Have variable skill sets. Somebody comes to you like, "Hey, I've got $1,500 if you write a couple pages of joke news clips this weekend!" Is your answer, "Sorry, I'm a serious writer of ghost stories that are meditations on sociological liminal spaces, in the novelette range, for far less money." Come on! Do the work and do it in a way that you can use to draw people into your existing work, figure out how to frame your publicity about it in a way that bolsters your connections to readers of ghost fiction about liminal spaces. Because, guess what? If you don't take the money it'll go to somebody else, maybe somebody who's less capable or deserving. It's okay and even necessary to take up space while building your reputation. And who knows? The person with joke article jobs today might be the editor of a speculative publishing imprint tomorrow.

These last two come purely from me, and I suppose they're tied together. The first half of this is to use your platform for community good. Boost other people and projects and even genres outside yours, or people and things well outside your wheelhouse like regional causes and so forth. People like people…that sounds a bit silly and obvious, but the context is that folks aren't into corporations, like publishers or music labels or production companies, as entities. Brands and branding? Yes. But, only in that we assign human characteristics to brands. So, be a person, three dimensional, with enough bones in your body to take a stance, even if it isn't the biggest life-or-death matter. If social media bots have more personality than you, people will start paying more attention to them instead of whatever you're promoting or building. Plus, the good will you engender by supporting others always comes back to you. The second part is: don't be a creep. Maybe "creep" is difficult to define, and maybe business isn't technically about social niceties, which tend to be ephemeral in nature anyway, but here's a good rule: if you wouldn't engage in a behavior on live TV and internet simulcast, where everyone is viewing you, maybe don't do it when you're engaging with people in the publishing scene. I'd say you should observe the Golden Rule, but this place is full of masochists, so…

N&M: You are a contemporary renaissance man, John. As a multi-media creator—writing, photography, musician, co-publisher, among others—how do they feed and inspire you across the mediums?

JEL: This has always been my process, although at the outset I had a singular focus on visual art. In early childhood, from kindergarten through sixth grade, I was considered gifted and talented when it came to drawing, painting, sculpture, etc. It was always great seeing my work on local television in the DC area—kids shows and the like, although I guess the actual news programs a couple times—and maybe that ingrained in me the notion it could be possible to create and have your creations taken seriously. During my teen years I was far too troubled to excel at school, but I did receive a dope Epiphone bass guitar for my birthday one year, and from that point on I've been in bands, recording demos, performing live. Listening to music had already become an integral part of focusing my attention for the creation of art, mostly comic books by that point, so it was a natural evolution. Side note: DC Comics gave excellent rejection letters to teenagers in the 1980s.

Like visual art, music was until recently too expensive for somebody to easily do on their own, so I took inventory and said, well, all I need to make it as a writer is a pen and paper. Over the years I had always composed stories or narrative games for the entertainment of my friends, and by my early twenties I was cranking out several pages a day anyway, so the progression was natural. Twenty-five years later it's more or less the same. Music for inspiration while writing, research during the writing process that inspires a song idea, photos that capture a mood or a moment I want paired with a story, or want to make an album cover with.

More than just bouncing back and forth between mediums I, at all times, have multiple tracks of music and plot running in the back of my mind simultaneously, generally one for composition and one for analysis of existing work by others. So, maybe four tracks of thought dedicated to music and writing operating in the background around the clock? Sounds distracting, and I suppose it is to an extent, but after so many decades I'm used to working around it.

N&M: Across all the mediums you work in, what do you think is your distinct "John Lawson" trademark/auteur element?

JEL: Well, you'll find several recurrent themes, or aesthetic hallmarks, spanning across my work. First and foremost, I'm enamored with the idea of "everyday darkness" as both realism and a speculative device. This can be used to amplify another of my focal points, the marginalized surreal. On top of which there is omnipresent failure. All three of which are most easily embodied by industrial decay. My hope is to convey the futility—and resultant despair—of attempting to live among other people in contemporary society. To my mind, we are trapped by the slow motion, crushing death that is the trash compactor formed by the poor choices of our past, and the poor outcomes of those choices coalescing into our future. More importantly, as a creative tool industrial decay is ubiquitous and multi-faceted. Characters can have jobs oriented around industrial decay, or it can define environments in stories, and won't be out of place as background noise—banging, clanging, gears grinding, screeches and implosions and so forth. Industrial accidents explain personal tragedies and social dynamics and policies, and audiences won't question it because industrial accidents, while tragic, are mundane. Commonplace. Need a reason for the menace, be it monster or deadly disease outbreak? The marvels of industrial decay help here as well. What is a pandemic in the age of enlightenment if not the everyday darkness of failure, surreal, and impacting the marginalized most of all? This is easy enough to capture in photography, and maybe music, but takes a bit more practice in fiction and screenplays—if for no other reason than we train ourselves to filter out all the imperfections in our environment.

N&M: How has your experience over the decades shaped and evolved your writing, music, and photography? How have the events of the past two years influenced/impacted your creative output?

JEL: Roughly a decade ago I experienced an extinction-level loss of work in progress and archived work when my old computer died, and the backups failed. It was the nightmare scenario creators in the digital age dread, but the experience was the crash course necessary to prep me for writing through a whole dark age and three supposed end of days, otherwise known as an election cycle and multistage pandemic.

Late 2019 and early 2020 saw me descend into a string of severe illnesses, some of which I'm still suffering the effects of, alongside having more work to do than ever before due to all of my various creative outlets taking off. This required working ever quicker and quicker, refining my personal methods, researching and learning new productivity techniques and incorporating all sorts of apps into my schedule. To be honest, I've been unable to accomplish any deep concentration work, like completing novels, going on two years now. What minuscule moments of solitude come my way are necessary for maintaining my health first and foremost, and creative work is squeezed in around the edges when possible. Again, the arts are akin to a battle of attrition. Live to art another day.

Which brings career priorities to the fore. It all comes down to this: what I would be unhappy dying without accomplishing? Aside from this obvious...living even more fulfilling years with my loved ones, and everything else we need as humans. As creators we always have our projects in the back of our minds that are, you know, "One day! One day I'll be able to do that wonderful thing, but I have to jump through X, Y, and Z hoops first!" Forget that. Do what you drives you now, don't let it wither away before you get to it.

N&M: How do you re-energize your creativity? Or, how do you stay motivated?

JEL: Staying creatively energized has had the biggest learning curve for me over the course of my career. Recognizing the physical limits of the hustle, the need to disengage and deescalate when it comes to chaos, negativity, and people who chronically derail whatever you're doing, I've had to learn about all this the hard way too many times. The investment in my physical and mental wellbeing has done more to bolster my creativity in the long run than anything else, because I've been through burn out, seen what it's like to take twenty-five times longer putting together a sentence when my brain is foggy, and have become discouraged and unmotivated because of it all.

Communication with peers, the good folks of the horror scene, is a must. Setting up virtual co-working spaces via Broadkill Writers' Resort and AllAccessCon has been a blessing. Listen, if there's something you want the scene to benefit from, that you want to benefit from, you've got to barge in and either help somebody make it happen, or do it yourself. Terraforming the horror space has always been a necessity, more so now than ever. Not only can you solve a problem for yourself, you build up the know-how and achievement of doing so. There are so many ways to build momentum if you just take a minute to get involved.

One other thing that helps is to remind myself of who I am, of the things I've done. It's easy to forget after a while where you began. All the cool things you wanted to do when you started down this creative path, and the things you actually ended up doing? Go back and revel in it once in a while. Like, I was just posting online how it just occurred to me the number of my poems that have been adapted into short films, and the number of award-winning short films by other writers I was involved in producing. That was for sure one of the things I used to sit around wishing would happen in my life. These days, here I am sitting around thinking, "Man, nothing ever happens," or, "Bummer I never got to do X, Y, or Z things," without acknowledging the short films, my novels, the hundreds of books I've helped authors publish, my book tours and awards and radio appearances and, well, you get the drift. It's like, calm down and just go do the work. It has value, it gets out there, just enjoy it.

N&M: Your seventh poetry collection, *Bibliophobia*, has just been released. What was the genesis of this collection and what do you want to accomplish with it?

JEL: One aspect of collections by other poets I admire, such as those of Stephanie M. Wytovich, that eluded me over the years was crafting a themed book from the ground up. The poems of *Bibliophobia* were written specifically for the purpose of being published together, whereas my past collections were written and published all over the place without a plan, then collected. As far as my previous collections go, I already did books skewed more toward long or short form works, like how *SuiPsalms* tends to go big, and more genre-specific work like in *The Horrible*.

Phobias are a huge personal and creative drive, while being universally relatable. This permits me to explore subjects that often go unexplored, or revisit familiar subjects in a completely unexpected way. The process has been long, eight years of piecing *Bibliophobia* together bit by bit, but I have been multitasking somewhat during that time, so I hope readers will forgive the delay. The idea for the collection came from Raw Dog Screaming Press striking a larger distribution deal for the library sector, and there were talks about reaching large audiences, which lead to thinking in terms of, well, if I were to build a poetry collection with intentionality, what could I do to reach a larger audience? What cohesive, unifying theme can I run with? That I landed on phobias as some sort of golden goose really cracks me up when I think back on it.

N&M: What can we look forward to seeing and hearing from you in the future?

JEL: Moving forward, you can expect a broader offering of products as I branch out. My friends and colleagues in the scene have inspired me to, first, deliver presentations at academic conferences, then teach workshops, and now publish papers and a longer examination of zombies — something I've been working on privately for my own amusement since 2009. It's really cool to have that project filtering out to the public after all this time, and to receive such a positive response! Beyond that, I've returned to screenplays. I'm not sure how much more I can say about that for the time being.

In the meantime, podcasting is something I've wanted to do for a while now, and I'm fortunate to be able to launch several in rapid succession, like *The Book Autopsy*, or *Genre Blackademia* with Rhonda J. Garcia, among others. The serial audio dramas of my fiction, and the poetry reading series, those might be a little more production intensive, but totally worth it. And easy enough to shoehorn in alongside the Rage Inducer album *A Torture Chamber Story*, with the album's maxi-singles "Broken Bones," "The Kindness of Strangers," and "Uncle Tom's Stabbin."

Last, but certainly not least, is the Netflix-style streaming app! Of everything here I'm most excited about this one. After all the effort to cultivate a deep catalogue of interviews, readings, panels, and other types of exclusive content through AllAccessCon since November 2019, we are able to offer an extension of the experience for those outside our live events. Plenty of original content not seen in our previous events can be found in the app as well. One of the good things to emerge from these past few years is the ability of technology to level the playing field for indie businesspeople. I hope it lives up to the expectations of our audience, and helps the horror scene continue expanding.

More information about John Lawson is available on his Raw Dog Screaming Press author page at http://rawdogscreaming.com/authors/john-edward-lawson/.

JENNIFER McMAHON

StokerCon® 2022 Guest of Honor

JENNIFER McMAHON is the *New York Times* Bestselling author of eleven novels, including *Promise Not to Tell, The Winter People,* and her latest, *The Children on the Hill.* She wrote her first short story, *The Haunted Meatball,* in third grade and has been filling notebooks with creepy stories ever since. She has written about ghosts, serial killers, evil fairies, haunted places and objects, and monsters real and imagined. She lives in Vermont with her partner, Drea, and their daughter, Zella.

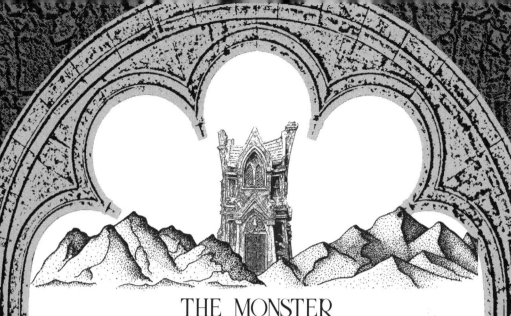

THE MONSTER

Excerpt from The Children on the Hill *by Jennifer McMahon*

August 15, 2019

Her smell sends me tumbling back through time to *before*.

Before I knew the truth.

It's intoxicating, this girl's scent. She smells sweet with just a touch of something tangy and sharp, like a penny held on your tongue.

I can smell the grape slushy she had this afternoon, the cigarettes she's been sneaking, the faint trace of last night's vodka (pilfered from her daddy's secret bottle kept down in the boathouse—I've watched them both sneak out to take sips from it).

She smells dangerous and alive.

And I love her walk—the way each step is a bounce like she's got springs at the bottoms of her feet. Like if she bounces high enough, she'll go all the way up to the moon.

The moon.

Don't look at the moon, full and swollen, big and bright.

Wrong monster. I am no werewolf.

Though I tried to be once.

Not long after my sister and I saw *The Wolf Man* together, we found a book on werewolves with a spell in it for turning into one.

"I think we should do it," my sister said.

"No way," I told her.

"Don't you want to know what it feels like to change?" she asked.

We sneaked out into the woods at midnight, did a spell under the full moon, cut our thumbs, drank a potion, burned a candle, and she was right— it was an exquisite thrill, imagining that we were turning into something so much more than ourselves. We ran naked and howling through the trees, pretending ferns were wolfsbane and eating them up.

We thought we might become the real thing, not like Lon Chaney Jr., with the wigs and rubber snout and yak hair glued to his face (my sister and I read that in a book too— "poor yaks," we said, giggling, guffawing about how bad that hair must have smelled).

When nothing happened that night, we were so disappointed. When we didn't sprout fur and fangs or lose our minds at the sight of the moon. When we went back home and swore to never speak of what we'd done as we pulled on our pajamas and crawled into our beds, still human girls.

"Can you guess what I am?" I ask the girl now. I don't mean to. The words just come shooting out like sparks popping up from a fire.

"Uh," she says, looking at me all strange. "I don't know. A ghost? Someone who was once a human bean?"

And that's just how she says it. Bean. Like we're all just baked beans in a pot, or maybe bright multicolored jelly beans, each a different flavor.

I'd be licorice. The black ones that get left at the bottom of the bag. The ones no one can stand the taste of.

I shift from one foot to the other, bits of my disguise clanking, rattling, the hair from the tangled wig I wear falling into my eyes.

I love this girl so much right now. All that she is. All that I will never be. All that I can never have.

And mostly, what I love is knowing what's coming next: knowing that I will change her as I've changed so many others.

I am going to *save* this girl.

"When do I get my wish?" she asks now.

"Soon," I say, smiling.

I am a giver of wishes.

A miracle worker.

I can give this girl what she most desires, but she isn't even aware of her own desires.

I can't wait to show her.

"So, do you want to play a game or something?" she asks.

"Yes," I say, practically shouting. *Yes, oh yes, oh yes!* This is my favorite question, my favorite thing! I know games. I play them well.

"Truth or dare?" she asks.

"If you wish. But I have to warn you, I'll know if you're lying."

She shrugs, tugs at her triple-pierced right earlobe, squints at me through all her layers of black goth makeup; a good girl trying so hard to look bad. "Nah. Let's play tag," she says, and this surprises me. She seems too old for such games. "My house is safety. You're it." Already running, she slaps my arm so hard it stings. I laugh. I can't help it. It's nerves. It's the thrill. There's no way this girl, with her stick-thin legs and cigarette smoke–choked lungs, can outrun me. I am strong. I am fast. I have trained my whole life for these moments.

I'm running, running, running, chasing this beautiful girl in the black hoodie, her blond hair with bright purple tips flying out behind her like a flag from a country no one's ever heard of. A girl so full of possibility, and she doesn't even know it. She's running, she's squealing, thinking she's going to make it back to safety, back to the bright lights of her little cabin that are just now coming into view through the trees (only bright because of the low hum of the generator out back, no power lines way out here). Thinking she's actually going to make it home, back to her parents (whom she hates) and her warm bed with the flannel sheets, back to her old dog, Dusty, who growls whenever he catches my scent—he knows what I am.

I have weeds woven into my hair. I am covered in a dress of bones, sticks, cattail stalks, old fishing line and bobbers. I am my own wind chime, rattling as I run. I smell like the lake, like rot and ruin and damp forgotten things.

I can easily overtake this girl. But I let her stay ahead. I let her hold on to the fantasy of returning to her old life. I watch her silhouette bounding through the trees, flying, floating.

And just like that, I'm a kid again, chasing my sister, pretending to be some movie monster (I'm the Wolf Man, I'm Dracula, I'm the Phantom of the motherfucking Opera) but I was never fast enough to catch her.

But I'm going to catch this girl now.

And I'm a real monster now. Not just pretend.

I'm going to catch this girl now because I never could catch my sister.

Here it is, forty years later, and still it's always her I'm chasing.

A CONVERSATION WITH JENNIFER McMAHON
by Sumiko Saulson

SUMIKO SAULSON (SS): Congratulations on being a 2022 StokerCon® Guest of Honor! How did you feel when you first found out you were going to be a GOH this year?

JENNIFER McMAHON (JM): I was stunned. My first reaction was: *Me? Really?* It's such a huge honor! I cannot tell you how grateful and thrilled I am to be recognized by the community in such a big way!

SS: Last year StokerCon® was completely online. StokerCon® 2022, like many conventions these days as we gradually recover from the pandemic, is a hybrid in-person/online event. And like many authors, you've been doing a lot of online appearances. How do you feel about all of the online events, and about hybrid events? Are there ways that the online offerings are helpful that you think might continue once the pandemic is over?

JM: I have mixed feelings. On the one hand, I'm so grateful that we have the technology to be able to do these online events and reach people even when we all need to stay at home to be safe. And it's been such an important way to stay connected to our community!

I have a big book launch party with my local independent bookshop each time I have a new release. Doing it online was wonderful because people who never would have been able to make it to Montpelier, Vermont to celebrate with me could show up!

On the other hand, there is nothing like an in-person event. There is a chemistry in the room you just can't get online. I've missed that. I've really missed being face-to-face with writer friends, fans, booksellers and librarians; the unexpected connections, the shared drinks and treats, the hugs!

I think virtual events are here to stay, and it is wonderful to have the opportunity to connect with people far away in this format. But I am so excited to see folks live, in-person at bookstores and libraries and conferences in 2022.

SS: Clearly, you are very dedicated to the horror genre. I mean, you have "write what scares you" tattooed on your wrist. What was your journey like, in coming to a place where you were not only an author but specifically a horror writer?

JM: That's such a great question! I think I've always been drawn to the dark, creepy side of writing and reading. I studied poetry for years in college, then for a year in an MFA program. When I turned to fiction, my first three attempted novels were written the way I thought people expected me to write. They were character driven, "literary," and (in retrospect) boring as hell. When I sat down to write book four, I asked myself the question I should have asked myself along: "What's the book I most want to read?" And the answer came back loud and clear: *A ghost story.* And it made total sense. Something clicked: my lifetime of loving scary books and movies, my obsession with ghosts and haunted places—I could work that into my fiction!

I think that even as I wrote that ghost story (which became my first published novel, *Promise Not to Tell*) and the books that followed it, I didn't understand I was writing horror. I called my books "psychological suspense with a supernatural twist". I went to mystery and thriller conferences and often felt like the odd girl out because I was writing books about other-worldly things and trying to not just give people the twists and turns of a suspense novel, but wanting to leave them feeling genuinely unsettled and wondering what's out there in the dark. It was only when I started hanging out with other horror authors, attending horror events, that I really felt I met my people, my tribe. That's when I realized, hey, I think I've been quietly writing horror all along!

SS: You are not only known as a horror writer, but also for suspense... and for generally the same books. How does it feel to sit on the intersection of horror and suspense? Where do the two genres differ and converge for you? And are there any differences in the fandoms?

JM: Honestly, I'm not thinking about genre as I write—I'm just trying to write the best books I can, books I would want to read, which for me means stories full of twists and turns and things that go bump in the night. I would say all good horror is suspenseful; but not all suspense novels contain elements of horror, if that makes sense!

I do sometimes think of my books as being a gateway to the horror world. They are picked up and read by people in book clubs who usually read women's fiction and historical fiction, by mystery and suspense lovers, by people who love books with strong female characters—and I hear all the time: "I don't do scary books. I don't do horror. But I love your books!" And they get hooked. They write or come to events telling me they had to sleep with lights on, but can I please recommend more creepy books like mine? So great!

SS: You have written about both supernatural creatures and human monsters such as serial killers. Which kinds of monsters do you think are the scariest, and why?

JM: Oh, hands down, the human monsters. It's partly that even if you are unable to fully suspend disbelief when reading about shape-shifters or the undead, everyone knows that human monsters really do walk among us, and that even well-intentioned people are capable of terrible acts, or of looking the other way when terrible acts are committed.

There are so many horrific things that can't be conquered in real life (or at least feel as though they can't be conquered) but in horror fiction, we get to conquer them, whether it's a serial killer or a vengeful spirit. And it's a thrill to drag that thing under the bed out into the light and realize we have the skills to not only survive it, but to face it, conquer it maybe, kill it once and for all.

SS: According to your bio, you live in Vermont in a creepy old Victorian on a hill with my partner, Drea, and daughter, Zella, explore the dark Vermont woods and seek out haunted places. Do you find inspiration for your stories in your home, and the places you explore? And do you ever scare yourself while writing about scary places that remind you of the place where you live and/or write?

JM: Most of my books are set in Vermont, and I spend a lot of time in the woods, exploring little towns, abandoned places, buildings and bridges that are said to be haunted. I find inspiration all around me. And yes, I do scare myself all the time, both when I visit these places for research and inspiration, and then later, when I sit down to write. I'm exploring my own fears on the page: poking at them with sticks, teasing them, drawing them out and trying to name them and make sense of them—all while living in a place that inspires some of those fears!

SS: As you probably know, last June the HWA had its first-ever series of Pride interviews showcasing LGBTQ authors—as a way to help showcase the diversity in the writing world and normalize our existence in the writing community. As a best-selling out lesbian author, do you feel being out presented any particular challenges for you? Or was it always just "this is how it is going to be"?

JM: Yes, I loved seeing the Pride interviews!

I feel very lucky. I don't believe being an out lesbian has ever gotten in the way of my career. Thanks to the advocacy of LGBTQ folks in earlier generations, it never even occurred to me when I was first published in 2008 to try to obscure the fact that I'm a lesbian, and it was certainly never suggested that I do so by my agent or editors. Are there readers out there who might not pick up my books when/if they learn I'm married to a woman? I guess so? I honestly feel badly for people who are that narrow-minded—it's no loss to me. The bigger question is, is there an LGBTQ kid or adult out there not sure if they should come out, not sure how they fit into the world, still figuring it all out, and they pick up one of my books or come to an event, and realize 'Oh hey, this writer is a lesbian. She's out, and doing fine!'

SS: Last April, you came out with *The Drowning Kind*, a book about a cursed swimming pool. Buildings and places as the monster are a large part of the gothic horror genre. Do you think of *The Drowning Kind*, or any of your other stories, as a part of that genre? Why or why not?

JM: Oh, definitely! Again, it's not something I consciously set out to do, but place is such an important part of my work, and I do love a Gothic atmosphere. I think of the setting as another living, breathing character with its own secrets and agenda that profoundly influences the story and people in it. Often place is a key part of the origin of a story idea for me—the Devil's Hand rock formation in *The Winter People*, Hattie's Bog in *The Invited*, the Tower Motel in *The Night Sister*, and so on!

SS: What do you have coming down the pike that our readers can look forward to?

JM: I'm super excited to have a short story included in the HWA anthology, *Other Terrors*, which will be out later this summer and has some amazing contributors!

I have a couple of books I've been tinkering with, including one for younger readers. I'm not sure yet what my next book for adults will be, but I promise it'll be on the creepy side!

SHEREE RENÉE THOMAS

StokerCon® 2022 Guest of Honor

S HEREE RENÉE THOMAS is an award-winning fiction writer, poet, and editor. Her work is inspired by myth and folklore, music, natural science, and the genius of the Mississippi Delta. *Nine Bar Blues: Stories from an Ancient Future* (Third Man Books, May 2020), her fiction collection, was honored as 2021 Finalist for the Ignyte, Locus, and World Fantasy Awards. She is also the author of two multigenre/hybrid collections, *Sleeping Under the Tree of Life* (Aqueduct Press, July 2016), longlisted for the 2016 Otherwise Award and honored with a Publishers Weekly Starred Review and *Shotgun Lullabies* (Aqueduct January 2011). She has been honored with fellowships & residencies from the Millay Colony of the Arts, Bread Loaf Environmental, NYFA, the Wallace Foundation, Ledig House/ Art Omi, Blue Mountain, MemphisArts, Cave Canem Foundation, VCCA, Tennessee Arts Commission, and Smith College. She edited the World Fantasy-winning groundbreaking black speculative fiction anthologies, *Dark Matter* (Grand Central, 2000 and 2004) and is the first to introduce W.E.B. Du Bois's science fiction short stories. Her work is widely anthologized and appears in *The Big Book of Modern Fantasy* edited by Ann & Jeff VanderMeer (Vintage, 2020), *The Year's Best Dark Fantasy Vol. 2* edited by Paula Guran, *The Year's Best African Speculative Fiction.* She is the Associate Editor of the historic Black arts literary journal, *Obsidian: Literature & the Arts in the*

African Diaspora, founded in 1975 and is the Editor of *The Magazine of Fantasy & Science Fiction,* founded in 1949. She also writes book reviews for *Asimov's.* She was recently honored as a 2020 World Fantasy Award Finalist in the Special Award—Professional category for contributions to the genre and is the Co-Host of the 2021 Hugo Awards Ceremony at DisCon III in Washington, DC with Andrea Hairston. Sheree is the Guest of Honor of WisCon 45 and a Guest of Honor of StokerCon® 2022. She is a Marvel writer and contributor to the anthology, *Black Panther: Tales of Wakanda* edited by Jesse J. Holland (Titan, March 2021) and collaborated with Janelle Monáe on the artist's forthcoming fiction collection, *The Memory Librarian and Other Stories from Dirty Computer* (Harper Voyager, April 2022). *Africa Risen: A New Era of Speculative Fiction,* a new anthology she co-edited with Oghenechovwe Donald Ekpeki and Zelda Knight, is forthcoming from Tordotcom Publishing in 2022. A former New Yorker, she lives in her hometown, Memphis, Tennessee near a mighty river and a pyramid. Visit www.shereereneethomas.com.

BAREFOOT AND MIDNIGHT

by Sheree Renée Thomas

Three men emerged from darkness and walked to the edge of the wood, the scent of roses rising all around them. The moon hung like a broken jaw above the Memphis night. The school yard lay ahead, its wood fence disjointed and leaning. The fetid scent of wet grass, of mold and moss, floated on the evening wind from the bayou.

"You ready?" asked the first man, his face pock-marked, lips leering, eyes sullen.

"Light 'em up," replied the second. The third nodded his head and produced the gasoline.

They knew the children slept inside. No one had to tell them. The Freedmen's School in Gayoso's Flats was one of several humble buildings where the former slaves gathered to grasp what hope lay ahead for their futures. Most had no home but the damp, mosquito-infested fields surrounding the bayou. The school housed thirteen orphaned children, those who didn't even have a mother's lap to lay their little heads on.

When the fires calmed down and the bright red embers turned to ash, when the city grieved and grieved until it couldn't grieve anymore, Dusa

Dayan rose from the back pew of Beale Street First African Baptist Church and let the sounds of Doctor Watts's hymns usher her out the red door.

I heard the cry. I, I, I heard them cry.

The fire had burned the schoolhouse to the ground. All that remained were the crimson rose bushes. The roses, the first seeds the children had planted together. She could still see the faces of her students, not much younger than herself, their beautiful smiles, the lustrous brown skin, the determination in their eyes. She tried to make those memories replace the burnt, black splinters of bone that haunted her nights, the faces unrecognizable, lips pulled back in horror. And the cries that made her wake from sleep, her face covered in tears.

I heard the cry. I, I, I

Hidden in darkness, donated evening meals still covered in her basket, Dusa had heard every scream.

And now, like a visit from a long-forgotten friend, the story her grandmother told her many years ago became Dusa's only thought.

There, under the roots of the Lynching Tree, were the remains of countless members of Dusa's kinfolk and others. Unfortunate souls singled out and taken away in the cover of night. Under the blood-stained bows, innocents had dangled and danced, lifeless beneath the broad, twisting limbs. It was a dance no soul wished ever to witness, a struggle of spirit and flesh, of ropes and blades and fire, a litany to pain that you could never unsee.

In the darkness the mound looked too small, too well-shaped to be natural. Only visible to eyes who had seen hell and lived. Beneath the grass was the specter behind the stories, no one knew the origins of the legend, the haint whose soul was said to hover above Voodoo Fields.

Dusa placed her satchel on the dirt. She drew the hatchet from the twine at her waist and gripped a hardwood handle laced with ancient carvings. The tree loomed over the mound, casting shadows. The few surrounding weeds were scraggly, thick with drops of dew. The land around the tree was fallow, as if the blood-soaked earth refused to nourish natural life. Dusa circled the mound, hatchet in hand, then she hacked off a branch from the Lynching Tree. The wet blades of grass felt slick against her bare soles. The wind whipped and pricked at her naked flesh. Exposed to the biting night and all its appetites, she knew the few drops of blood would not be all of the sacrifice.

When she took the branch from the tree where no leaves or blossoms grew, the ground grumbled and growled beneath her feet. Dusa held her breath.

Barefoot and covered only in the darkness that was midnight, she shivered. On bent knees, she dug her fingers into the grass, grasping at the moist earth, clutched cherry bark and broken twigs, her back arched in pain. She lifted a flask, sprinkled bathwater from a child who was not baptized. Behind her the creek murmured and whispered, a cool invitation to abandon her mission. She could toss all the gathered items in the creek's dark waters, leave the terrors behind her. She could forget the tree and the cursed land that surrounded it, walk back through the red doors of the church, and beg for forgiveness.

Dusa rose on one knee, flask in hand, praying that she had the strength to turn her back on the Lynching Tree, but a fire burned in her soul. The faith she once had was replaced with an unholy rage, an anger so hot, it incinerated all forgiveness. She willed her body to move. But the scent of roses, overpowering in the night, strengthened her resolve, holding her there.

The fires were started by those who hated the very idea that any of them were now free. White Memphis defined itself by the darkness it kept outside of Freedom's light, by the darkness that festered within. The Freedmen's School was the only home Dusa had ever known. Frozen in winter, smoldering in summer, she and her thirteen students had suffered and struggled together as one. The bite of skeetas, the occasional serpent intruder were all well worth it. She had watched them, ages eight to fourteen, come through the old pine doors, eyes glistening with want for knowledge. The confidence on their faces emerged like spring blossoms as they slowly moved from signing their names with an X to the new names they had chosen for themselves in freedom.

But Voodoo Fields was where the ancient spirit lay, waiting. When no earthly justice would bring stolen Black lives peace. Dusa dug up the earth, the raw scent filling the air. She sprinkled the soil with her tears and pulled the ragged mud doll from its dreamless rest. Wrapped in tree roots, its garment was tattered. Whatever color or pattern it once held faded long ago. A dark, rust-colored stain covered the space where its heart should be. It had no head. It had no limbs. No mouth or plump cheeks and belly to kiss and pinch.

Dusa held a rose petal for every child she lost in the fire. She pressed them into the freshly made mud she used to cover the old doll. The mud spread like a second skin, the old layers, hard and cracking. As she held the doll, she thought she heard it cry out, the sound like a newborn baby hungry for its mother's milk. She nearly dropped it, but fear made her hold fast, the scream stuck in her throat.

The Lynching Tree branch smelled of smoke, fear, and blood. Pain radiated through her palms as she worked to fashion two arms, two legs, and a fist full of dark, earthwormed-soil for a head. She sculpted the head as roundly as she could in the darkness, resisted the urge to abandon the writhing ball of rotten soil. As she worked the doll felt heavier in her hand, like the child she once bore and buried before its first spring.

She sang the song before she realized she knew the song. In a language neither she nor her mother's tongue had ever sung before. Words that came from no leather-bound hymnal. Words that were dark, mournful, dangerous. It was the same song her grandmother sang before the spirit doll had slain the men who hung her husband, the same song she sang, they say, when the black doll came for her, too.

Hear I. Hear I cry. Rend them, spin them, hear them crying.

Dusa placed her palm flesh over the hatchet's blade and sang until her voice grew hoarse from crying. Her elbows were steady but arms wobbly. Her knees had grown numb, but the sharp scent of sweat, burned flesh, and urine made her squeeze the blood more rapidly into the doll's primitive mouth. No eyes were carved into the mud. The spirit doll needed only blood and the ashes of the dead to see.

Eyes stinging, Dusa held the doll to her bosom. She rocked and stroked it as she had once rocked her own child. Lulled by her mother's voice, the infant girl had gone to sleep one cold wintry night, but the child never opened her eyes again. Dusa was thinking of the baby's warm, fat fingers when she felt the mud doll's head shift in her hand. More corpse than baby, the doll once cold and still, began to writhe and twist in her arms. The fat, sightless grubs and earthworms burying through its mud-bottom flesh. A rotten smell, like spoiled vegetables and dead leaves, filled the air. Strange roots burst from the doll's center. Dusa dropped it and scrambled to her feet.

Hear I! Hear I cry!

The bayou moved around her. The Lynching Tree leaned left, now right. Its greatest branches twisted, as if reaching for the spirit Dusa had released from its sleep. A howling wind moved across the black waters, spreading the sound of wailing and the scent of long dead things. A great sound, timber fall and cracked limbs, roots twisting over the sour earth joined the endless drone of cicadas resting on the bark of the Lynching Tree.

Rend them! Spin them!

Dusa did not recognize her voice but she knew the cracked notes that joined hers was the root child now fully grown. Sightless, the creature rose on driftwood legs, the rags left in a pile in the cursed soil, the mound exposed, an open wound. Its bulbous head blocked the moonlight. Dusa could not tear her eyes away from its pitiful face. Earthworms writhed across its muddy skin in shifting waves, like water. The stench of terror, of lives cut short from rage, greed, and madness invaded all of her senses. Her voice now a whisper, but still she sang.

Hear them crying!

The mud doll towered over her, facing her as if awaiting instructions. *Cry!* Its voice growing stronger as the wind whipped bark from the Lynching Tree's limbs. *Cry! Hear I!*

Dusa raised her arm, the deep gash stung. She held the hatchet to the spirit doll. The blood from her palms emblazing the carved symbols in the handle, bright red suns and comet tails in a script that appeared in frightful dreams.

Red blossoms burst from the spirit doll's chest, sprouted along its limbs, and legs. Thorny vines twisted around its throat. Its rib cage was made of roots and twigs, splinters of charred bone, remnants of the Lynching Tree. It held the hatchet high and swung it.

News of the vicious killings spread faster than the fires that had lit the city's nights. For three whole days, white men's intestines hung from the Lynching Tree, the limbs heavy with the weight of strange fruit. To Dusa, the spilled guts looked like a string of bloody red rubies and pearls. How beautiful they looked, glistening in the sunlight. She wished she could wrap them around her throat like a necklace and dance. For three days she walked the streets of Memphis with the mud from the Lynching Tree dried on her feet, blood caked in the palm of her hand. On the fourth day Dusa walked barefoot through the ashes of the fallen school.

The wound had not healed.

She plucked a rose from a bush and drifted down to the bayou, in the same gown she'd worn since that first night beneath the Lynching Tree. The creek was placid, a black mirror, shimmering, calm. The dark water she touched was the last of what had passed and the first of what was to come. She washed mud from her fingernails, sprinkled the water over her eyes, a baptism, and waited for the doll to come for her, barefoot and midnight.

A CONVERSATION WITH SHEREE RENÉE THOMAS

by Linda D. Addison

I'm delighted to have this time to talk with you, Sheree. Our paths crossed for the first time in 2000, when you published my story in the first groundbreaking *Dark Matter* anthology of Black speculative fiction, which put my career on a wonderful trajectory.

Since then, you have been honored with awards as an editor and author and Guest of Honor at several major conventions, including co-hosting the 2021 Hugo Awards with novelist Andrea Hairston, in recognition of your impact on the field. Your fiction, poetry, and essays are a valued part of my inspiration and acknowledged by the field with awards, year's best lists, etc. Your writing has been translated in Spanish, French, and Urdu and included in too many anthologies and magazines for me to mention here (but readily available on your site www.shereereneethomas.com).

LINDA ADDISON (LA): You've talked about how the idea of the first *Dark Matter* anthology came to you. How did you feel as it began to receive such glowing reviews and awards? Did you know it would make such a huge impact in the field, spawning other African American anthologies like *Dark Thirst* (vampires), *Dark Dreams* (Horror and Suspense by Black Writers) and lifting little known authors (like myself) into the light?

SRT: Little known then, but beloved now! Bram Stoker Award and Pulitzer Prize winners, National Book Award finalists, and too many other honors to name, *Dark Matter*'s contributors have gone on to make history in so many ways, and it has been a joy to see, since, as you said, many weren't well-known voices in the field. I was just thinking about how contributor Pam Noles impacted the creation of *Lovecraft Country* or how others in the book have gone on to inspire so many writers we love today.

It's been twenty-four years since I started the research that would become *Dark Matter.* To say I foresaw any of the significant changes that have now become part of our field would be disingenuous. I knew that the work of excavation was vital and that the stories and writers were there, but I did not know how it would be received or what communities would spring up from the space we created.

Like many of the writers in the anthologies—Samuel R. Delany, Ishmael Reed, Walter Mosley, Steven Barnes and Tananarive Due, Kalamu ya Salaam, and the late Amiri Baraka, Wanda Coleman, and Charles R. Saunders—Octavia E. Butler was very supportive of the anthologies and the contributors to both volumes, *Dark Matter: A Century of Speculative Fiction from the African Diaspora* and *Dark Matter: Reading the Bones.* We'd met several times before I pitched the then unnamed anthology to her and before I would study with her at Clarion West in '99. I'd interviewed her at Yari Yari. She'd told me that she and Martin Greenberg had tried to publish an anthology, but were told by publishers that "no one wanted to read a book about race." We'd talked about how the very act of creating stories with Black characters as protagonists, the heroes in their own adventures and journeys, was perceived as being inherently political, making the entire work for some readers—and publishers— "about race."

It was a frustration that Butler, of course, handled graciously, by continuing to write kick-ass novels and stories that quieted that noise. The work was the work, and she did it masterfully. Knowing she still chose to people her stories and the worlds she created with not only Black women characters, resilient, caring, and sensible like the women in her family, but with diverse communities who faced extraordinary challenges, was important to see, and it made me appreciate the possibilities that a collection like *Dark Matter* could open up for everyone.

I was thrilled and not surprised to see other communities beginning to publish their work as well. Several volumes came out in addition to the delicious litany of *Dark ___* books. I think on these shores, Black people are used to opening doors that are closed to them, by symbolic force and sheer necessity—we're trying to live and prosper as well, you know—and when we break down those doors, everyone and their mama comes through right with us. Has it ever been different?

So here we are. Now everyone discusses W. E. B. Du Bois's work as science fiction—first introduced in the *Dark Matter* anthologies. And there isn't this assumption that Black writers don't exist in the field beyond the two or three people could name at the time. We have long been here and if you actually thought about it, you could have easily named many other fine writers and added them to the lists of those who create speculative fiction.

It's a thrilling contribution that never stops feeling new to me, because I remember the blank stares and the dismissiveness that came when people learned I was interested in science fiction, and even more so coming from someone non-white. Some things have changed wonderfully, and some things remain the same. It's cyclical, but with each round of negotiations and innovations we get a little closer to being able to experience this field and the publishing industry the way other writers do.

It's always been about perception—who is perceived as being 'universal' or 'present' (thank goodness we no longer have to debate about *mere existence*, as in, "do Black people read and write science fiction? *I dunno!*"). It's always been about who is 'valued' and what stories are worth supporting, worth being told. We didn't have a *Fiyah Magazine* then—so if your stories were perceived as too Black or too extra or whatever, you were ass out, *ha ha*! We didn't have the kind of social media we live and breathe today. So, community-building and even visualizing a possible critical mass was really hard. People weren't yet fully comfortable with reading and publishing short fiction online. Digital books weren't even part of the publishing boilerplate back then. *Strange Horizons* was first published two months after the first volume of *Dark Matter* appeared in hardcover. It was an exciting time full of possibility. None of us knew what the future might hold, but we were hopeful, and it feels like we are in the midst of that kind of change again.

LA: You excel as an editor, teacher, and a writer, how do you balance your time between working with others and doing your own writing?

SRT: Thank you, very kind of you, Linda! Balance is the goal, but sometimes you must be truly intentional. You have to carve out time for the things that truly matter to you, and for the other things just do your best. So, I don't know about achieving the most excellent balance all the time, but I do know that I am reclaiming my time as Aunty Waters once said.

When my children were younger, I experimented with writing at different times of the day—late at night at one point, then I switched to early mornings, before we did the off-to-school rumba. The point was to do it before anyone else in the house was conscious, and when interruptions would be less likely. So, I became a nocturnal being for reading and research, up at the devil's hour to actually write. I still don't know why it works, only that so far, long after those mothering years, it just does. And if that changes, I'll change again, because trusting your instincts and being flexible is a necessary survival tactic in this field. I'm much better at focusing on others' worlds after I've carved out that time for my own.

LA: Your fiction and poetry sing beautifully of earth magic and folklore, can you talk about where these influences come from?

SRT: Earth magic and folklore, natural science and music, all of those interwoven threads come from observation, faith, and practice. From being a witness to the magic of the world, the power of words, and the way our stories, even the oldest ones still linger with us and impact our psychology. I come from a spiritual people of deep faith and a lot of dark humor. That's how we survived the traumas and a nightmarish history in this world. But there was always light. Sometimes that was expressed in the church and sometimes that was expressed elsewhere, in the world and in the art, and just in living.

There's a sense of greater things, definitely more powerful than we as a species may ever truly understand, but the mystery won't stop us from trying to do so. It's that mystery and magic, that weirdness that makes me curious, and it's something I lean into and explore when it feels right. Backsliders and Scripture-quoters, the let-it-be-what-it's-gon'-be folks, all of those ways of seeing and being are important in recreating or reimagining the world on the page. There's something powerful and frightening in all of it, in the old haints and too-horrible-but-its-true tales that my grandfather and his friends, neighbors would share. I think it's no coincidence that the Black horror we are seeing today explores how the very act of us existing is often the source of the horror. Blackness in these films and series is the catalyst, the motivating force and that's been true in more ways than we like to tell, but that's the real scary stuff. Beacons in the journey included Zora and Walker, Morrison and Jones, Dumas, Reed, Baraka and Bradbury, Garcia and Rushdie, so many writers whose writing transported me, sparked my imagination.

LA: You've mentioned in other interviews that your father was a true music lover and listened to all kinds of music. Do you think this impacted your writing style, which I find very lyrical? Have you ever played an instrument?

SRT: Remember that scene from the end of *Raiders of the Lost Ark?* When the warehouse worker pushes the hand truck carrying the ark in a crate? When the camera pans out to reveal that the ark is just one of hundreds, maybe even thousands of mysterious artifacts stashed away and forgotten? Well, imagine crates of albums and that was my dad's record collection. A child's imagination! My dad was a musician when he was in high school, and I still remember him playing his guitar when I was younger. My dad's walk was music and I still love it, even though now he's got extra swag with his cane. My parents loved music and they passed that on to us. There are some years of life that I call up just by the album cover—a whole soundtrack and mood.

Music, storytelling, not only informs my work; it's the birth of my work—the oral storytelling from my family and elders, the music legends that are in the family and inspired and brought a lot of hope to the most non-musical family members like myself. Born in Eden, Mississippi, Son Thomas, a bluesman and sculptor used to make skulls out of clay. "We all end up in the clay" is what they say he said, but he actually meant something else.

Isaac Hayes made history when he became the third African American to win an Oscar, after Hattie McDaniel and Sidney Poitier. He was only twenty-nine years old, and he took my great-grandmother Rushia Taylor Wade as his date. That Oscar was in grandmama's house in North Memphis for years. Now it's at the Stax Museum. So, when it comes to music, our family's full of talented folks, has some great people who really do that, but I knew I wasn't going to be one of them, heh! Can't sing at'tall!

But I could write. And starting out, I knew I didn't want to write works that were constantly translating to a mainstream audience. I could just imagine my brothers or my cousins reading a line and thinking, wait, you felt the need to explain that? You can't half tell the story because you're stopping to make asides and fill folks on, when your own folks already know what time it is. I wanted to learn how to balance the things that are intrinsic to a culture while inviting spaces for others to come in. When I started being in workshop spaces, I saw some writers struggling to filter out those things that made them stand out (in my humble opinion), in an effort to show how good they were at mimicking, trying to assimilate and fit in.

In our country, you're given many opportunities to learn those patterns and those rhythms. They don't need me to repeat what they've already seen and heard. I wanted to write stories, that if you listen with your inner ear, you might hear some other new, interesting things, too. The main thing those early models taught me, from Hayes to Hurston, Dumas and Du Bois, is that yes, we have our own stories, and they are worth telling.

Music is a muse and that is evident throughout my debut fiction collection, *Nine Bar Blues: Stories from an Ancient Future*. The stories cross genres, cross time, and geographies, but the threads that unite them are music, Memphis, and maybe, a case could be made for insects. Music is like the air we breathe in the city, and I don't think that's an exaggeration. Folks really do love their music in Memphis, and it's a special place in that regard, because you can hear music from various eras. For me as a creator, there is usually a soundtrack of some kind playing in the background while I am pre-writing, researching, or laying down the bones of my next work. Sometimes that soundtrack is curated specifically for a project I'm working on. I already know the music that my characters are listening to, or the sounds that impact and shape their lives. Other times it's white noise. But everything is silence when I reach the end. It's a different zone, especially during revisions, and at that time, I am just alone with the words and my own thoughts.

LA: In the last couple of years work edited and created by African authors/editors is getting recognition. How did you become involved, as an editor with Oghenechovwe Donald Ekpeki and Zelda Knight, with the anthology *Africa Risen: A New Era of Speculative Fiction* being released in 2022 by Tordotcom Publishing?

SRT: *Africa Risen* is the book I would have edited back in '98 and '99 if the world was different. I didn't have a large footprint then—the contributors trusted me with their work even though I wasn't a *name* they could pull off their personal shelves. They believed in the work and the project and had faith in the possibility it represented. Forever grateful for that leap of faith, from writers known and relatively unknown at the time. But Nnedi Okorafor was one of the few African / Nigerian American writers who consciously and unapologetically wrote science fiction and fantasy with Black people and culture as its focus. Peter Kalu in the UK was publishing novels as well. They were proud to create work in the genre, and that wasn't something you could say about a lot of others at the time. The attitudes from some people outside the genre ranged from mild surprise or incredulity to outright dismissiveness. Today, it is not uncommon to see Black writers, where African or from her diaspora, included on the awards lists, but that certainly not the case when I entered the field. I was excited to include works by the Canadian, Caribbean, and UK authors in *Dark Matter*. Now I'm happy to say that Leone Ross, a contributor to the first volume of *Dark Matter* has edited a new volume of Black British speculative fiction that will be coming out soon from Peepal Tree Press.

LA: The landscape of speculative writing and publishing has become more diverse since 2000, what do you think has led to these changes in the last twenty years, what do you feel is left to be done?

SRT: That's a whole sermon, a keynote address, and I don't have the bandwidth for it now, lol. But I will say that people—writers and readers—aren't really buying the "we don't know who the audience is…don't know how to market it" lines anymore. Since the work that Walter Mosley spearheaded back when we were on the PEN Open Book committee, trying to get more diversity in actual paid jobs in book publishing, to all of the various conversations and educational work that so many writers and supporters of the genre have been doing over the years, including organizations like the Carl Brandon Society and the Otherwise Awards, etc., there is a lot of forces that have been in play.

Black cultural innovations come from the underground, from the margins, and we're going to do our thing, whether the mainstream notices it or not. By the time they do, we've been doing that thing for quite some time and have already started innovating something else. None of that means our work is done and that we have arrived at the promised land. People still talk about diversity as if it is an uprising in the fields. We're still patting ourselves on the back as an industry, checking off boxes without actually engaging with what it means in real-time to invite others into these spaces. I'm thinking about what it really means to show up and how that reception isn't always what the Con brochures say it is. The same is true now as it was then—you need more voices at the table and those voices need to be empowered and listened to.

I am proud to witness the publication of *Sycorax's Daughters,* the landmark Black women's horror anthology you co-edited with Kinitra Brooks PhD and Susana Morris PhD, and the Horror Noire documentary and film series Tananarive Due helped usher into the canon. These contributions are creating more possibilities in the field, highlighting wonderful work.

When agents and publishers feel like they can handle publishing more than one _____ (fill in the blank with your choice) writer at a time, then we're inching our way towards more progress. I'm looking forward to the days when it isn't exceptional to see more than a handful of writers in our field who have actual careers. The time when the work is regarded as integral and vital, and supported as such, and not as temporary trends, that cycles in and out as the nation's conscience dictates.

Every awards table of contents should be brimming with diverse voices. I shouldn't be able to pick out the one or two Indigenous or Black writer or whomever, because they're that rare. The year's best volumes and lists need to do more than *mention* this work. Too much excellent work is being written and published, and you're going to miss me with the blatant absences. I mean really. We notice and we see it and there is no excuse. There are so many new, talented people entering the field, writers *already* contributing to the field— and you can't count them all on your hands, so that is definitely something to remain hopeful and excited about, but yes, there is more work to be done, and it isn't just by us.

LA: What other projects are coming out in the future, in addition to the anthology *Africa Risen: A New Era of Speculative Fiction?*

SRT: Pan Morigan, Troy L. Wiggins, and I are thrilled to share *Trouble the Waters: Tales of the Deep Blue,* a volume of wonderful water-themed stories from gifted, global writers. That's out now and published by Third Man Books. I'm also thrilled to have collaborated with the amazing artist Janelle Monáe on the novelet, "Timebox Altar(ed)," in her debut fiction collection, *The Memory Librarian and Other Stories of Dirty Computer,* from HarperCollins/Harper Voyager. I am publishing more horror (and poetry!) in *The Magazine of Fantasy & Science Fiction,* so that's been great, look for that work and write about it if you can. I also have some stories coming out in other anthologies and a special project that is not announced yet. I am doing a wee happy dance inside just thinking about it, so let me stop now, because I'm about to burst with this good news. And I am very grateful to have good news in these strange times, because when the pandemic began, it felt like the world was ending. One thing to imagine, quite another to experience it. So, with that, may we all continue moving onward, striving and imagining new adventures together!

THE 2021 BRAM STOKER AWARDS®
FINAL BALLOT

SUPERIOR ACHIEVEMENT IN A NOVEL

Castro, V. - *The Queen of the Cicadas* (Flame Tree Press)

Hendrix, Grady - *The Final Girl Support Group* (Berkley)

Jones, Stephen Graham - *My Heart Is a Chainsaw* (Gallery/Saga Press)

Pelayo, Cynthia - *Children of Chicago* (Agora Books)

Wendig, Chuck - *The Book of Accidents* (Del Rey)

SUPERIOR ACHIEVEMENT IN A FIRST NOVEL*

Martinez, S. Alessandro - *Helminth* (Omnium Gatherum)

McQueen, LaTanya - *When the Reckoning Comes* (Harper Perennial)

Miles, Terry - *Rabbits* (Del Rey)

Piper, Hailey - *Queen of Teeth* (Strangehouse Books)

Quigley, Lisa - *The Forest* (Perpetual Motion Machine Publishing)

Willson, Nicole - *Tidepool* (The Parliament House)

*Due to a tie in fifth place, there are six nominees in this category.

SUPERIOR ACHIEVEMENT IN A GRAPHIC NOVEL

Ahmed, Saladin (author) and Kivelä, Sami (artist) - *Abbott 1973* (BOOM! Studios)

Garcia, Kami (author); Suayan, Mico (artist); Badower, Jason (artist); and Mayhew, Mike (artist) - *Joker/Harley: Criminal Sanity* (DC Comics)

Manzetti, Alessandro (author) and Cardoselli, Stefano (artist) - *The Inhabitant of the Lake* (Independent Legions Publishing)

Morrison, Grant (author); Child, Alex (author); and Franquiz, Naomi (artist) - *Proctor Valley Road* (BOOM! Studios)

Panosian, Dan (author) and Ignazzi, Marianna (artist) - *An Unkindness of Ravens* (BOOM! Studios)

SUPERIOR ACHIEVEMENT IN A YOUNG ADULT NOVEL

Blake, Kendare - *All These Bodies* (Quill Tree Books)

Boyle, R.L. - *The Book of the Baku* (Titan Books)

Lewis, Jessica - *Bad Witch Burning* (Delacorte Press)

Sutherland, Krystal - *House of Hollow* (G.P. Putnam's Sons)

Waters, Erica - *The River Has Teeth* (HarperTeen)

SUPERIOR ACHIEVEMENT IN LONG FICTION

Castro, V. - *Goddess of Filth* (Creature Publishing, LLC)

Khaw, Cassandra - *Nothing But Blackened Teeth* (Tor Nightfire)

LaRocca, Eric - *Things Have Gotten Worse Since We Last Spoke* (Weirdpunk Books)

Piper, Hailey - "Recitation of the First Feeding" (*Unfortunate Elements of My Anatomy*) (The Seventh Terrace)

Strand, Jeff - "Twentieth Anniversary Screening" (*Slice and Dice*) (Independently published)

Superior Achievement in Short Fiction

Gyzander, Carol - "The Yellow Crown"

(*Under Twin Suns: Alternate Histories of the Yellow Sign*) (Hippocampus Press)

Murray, Lee - "Permanent Damage" (*Attack From the '80s*) (Raw Dog Screaming Press)

O'Quinn, Cindy - "A Gathering at the Mountain"

(*The Bad Book*) (Bleeding Edge Books)

Taborska, Anna - "Two Shakes Of A Dead Lamb's Tail"

(*Terror Tales of the Scottish Lowlands*) (Telos Publishing)

Ward, Kyla Lee - "A Whisper in the Death Pit" (Weirdbook #44) (Wildside Press)

Superior Achievement in a Fiction Collection

Files, Gemma - *In That Endlessness, Our End* (Grimscribe Press)

Fracassi, Philip - *Beneath a Pale Sky* (Lethe Press)

Maberry, Jonathan - *Empty Graves: Tales of the Living Dead* (WordFire Press LLC)

Tuttle, Lisa - *The Dead Hours of Night* (Valancourt Books)

Wise, A.C. - *The Ghost Sequences* (Undertow Publications)

Superior Achievement in a Screenplay

Chaisson, C. Henry; Antosca, Nick; and Cooper, Scott - *Antlers* (Searchlight Pictures)

Dong-hyuk, Hwang - *Squid Game*, Season 1,

Episode 1: "Red Light, Green Light" (Siren Pictures)

Flanagan, Mike; Flanagan, James; and Howard, Jeff - *Midnight Mass,* Season 1,

Episode 6: "Book VI: Acts of the Apostles" (Intrepid Pictures)

Graziadei, Phil and Janiak, Leigh - *Fear Street: Part One - 1994* (Chernin Entertainment)

Peele, Jordan; Rosenfeld, Win; and DaCosta, Nia - *Candyman* (Universal Pictures)

SUPERIOR ACHIEVEMENT IN A POETRY COLLECTION

Lansdale, Joe R. - *Apache Witch and Other Poetic Observations* (Independent Legions Publishing)

McHugh, Jessica - *Strange Nests* (Apokrupha)

Simon, Marge and Turzillo, Mary - *Victims* (Weasel Press)

Sng, Christina; Yuriko Smith, Angela; Murray, Lee; and Flynn, Geneve - *Tortured Willows: Bent. Bowed. Unbroken.* (Yuriko Publishing)

Snyder, Lucy A. - *Exposed Nerves* (Raw Dog Screaming Press)

SUPERIOR ACHIEVEMENT IN AN ANTHOLOGY

Chambers, James - *Under Twin Suns: Alternate Histories of the Yellow Sign* (Hippocampus Press)

Datlow, Ellen - *When Things Get Dark: Stories Inspired by Shirley Jackson* (Titan Books)

French, Aaron J. and Landry, Jess - *There is No Death, There are No Dead* (Crystal Lake Publishing)

Guignard, Eric J. - *Professor Charlatan Bardot's Travel Anthology to the Most (Fictional) Haunted Buildings in the Weird, Wild World* (Dark Moon Books)

Johnson, Eugene - *Attack From the '80s* (Raw Dog Screaming Press)

SUPERIOR ACHIEVEMENT IN NON-FICTION

Knost, Michael - *Writers Workshop of Horror 2* (Hydra Publications)

Olson, Danel - *9/11 Gothic: Decrypting Ghosts and Trauma in New York City's Terrorism Novels* (Lexington Books)

Weinstock, Jeffrey Andrew and Hansen, Regina M. - *Giving the Devil His Due: Satan and Cinema* (Fordham University Press)

Wetmore Jr., Kevin J. - *Eaters of the Dead: Myths and Realities of Cannibal Monsters* (Reaktion Books)

Woofter, Kristopher - *Shirley Jackson: A Companion* (Peter Lang Publishing)

SUPERIOR ACHIEVEMENT IN SHORT NON-FICTION

Ognjanović, Dejan - "The Three Paradigms of Horror"
(Vastarien Vol. 4, Issue 2) (Grimscribe Press)

O'Quinn, Cindy - "One and Done"
(*Were Tales: A Shapeshifter Anthology*) (Brigids Gate Press)

Verona, Emily Ruth - "A Horror Fan's Guide to Surviving Womanhood"
(thefinalgirls.co.uk)

Wetmore Jr., Kevin J. - "Devil's Advocates: The Conjuring"
(Auteur Publishing/Liverpool University Press)

Yuriko Smith, Angela - "Horror Writers: Architects of Hope"
(The Sirens Call, Halloween 2021, Issue 55) (Sirens Call Publications)

StokerCon

Lifetime Achievement Awards

JO FLETCHER
NANCY HOLDER
KOJI SUZUKI

THE HWA LIFETIME ACHIEVEMENT AWARD

The HWA is proud to announce our Lifetime Achievement Award winners: JO FLETCHER, NANCY HOLDER, and KOJI SUZUKI. Their awards will be given at this year's StokerCon®, happening in Denver, Colorado in May.

The Lifetime Achievement Award is presented periodically to an individual whose work has substantially influenced the horror genre. While this award is often presented to a writer, it may also be given for influential accomplishments in other creative fields.

The Lifetime Achievement Award is the most prestigious of all awards presented by HWA. It does not merely honor the superior achievement embodied in a single work. Instead, it is an acknowledgement of superior achievement in an entire career.

Congratulations to this year's recipients!

LIFETIME ACHIEVEMENT AWARD RECIPIENT
JO FLETCHER

J O FLETCHER lives in Northeast London, England. She is the founder
and publisher of Jo Fletcher Books, and UK publisher Quercus' specialist
horror, fantasy, and science fiction imprint. She is also a writer, ghost-
writer and occasional poet, following earlier careers as a local, then Fleet
Street journalist (once commended by a High Court judge for helping stop a
bomber), and a film and book critic. She's been published widely, both in and
out of horror, fantasy, and science fiction. She has won awards for her writing
and services to the genre, including the World Fantasy, the British Fantasy
Society's August Derleth and the International Society of Poets Awards.

Jo's publishing career began in the late 1970s, when she began co-running
the British Fantasy Society, and was a regular contributor to *Science Fiction
Chronicle*, amongst other periodicals. She is one of the founding members
of the Horror Writers Association, and has been a trustee, sits on the board
of the World Fantasy Convention, and is a member of the World Fantasy
Awards Administration. Jo co-chaired several British FantasyCons, as well as
the 1988 and 1997 World Fantasy Conventions in London.

Jo's publishing career started in 1985 when she joined the brand-new
indie publisher Headline, introducing horror greats like Charles L. Grant,
Chet Williamson and Dan Simmons to the British reading public. A short

stint at Mandarin (Hamlyn)—and a chance to republish the entire Dennis Wheatley oeuvre—was followed by several years at the newly revitalized genre list at Pan Macmillan, where her authors included Charles de Lint, Richard Christian Matheson and Graham Joyce, as well as *Dark Voices: The Pan Book of Horror* anthology series. After a short stint at Penguin, working on the brief-lived horror imprint Signet, she moved to Gollancz, then an independent publisher, to run the genre list there, and stayed as it became part of the Hachette UK empire under Orion. Additionally, she founded the Fantasy Masterworks list to sit alongside the Science Fiction Masterworks. Her authors ranged from old masters like H.P. Lovecraft and Robert E. Howard to bestselling and award-winning masters like Terry Pratchett, Ursula K. Le Guin, Andrzej Sapkowski and Charlaine Harris, to new discoveries like Joe Hill, Tom Lloyd and Ben Aaronovitch, as well as the award-winning *Dark Terrors* series.

In 2011 Quercus, then a young independent publisher, lured her away to start Jo Fletcher Books. Jo Fletcher Books returned to the Hachette stable in 2014 when Hodder acquired Quercus. Jo Fletcher Books continues Jo's tradition of publishing some of the very best writers in the interconnected fields of horror, fantasy, and science fiction. Current authors range widely across the field, from Silvia Moreno-Garcia, Alison Littlewood, Amal El-Mohtar, Max Gladstone, to newcomers like Ry Herman and Breanna Teintze.

In her rare spare time, Jo sings, mostly classical choral music, gardens, watches birds, and cooks. www.jofletcherbooks.com

LIFETIME ACHIEVEMENT AWARD RECIPIENT
NANCY HOLDER

New York Times bestselling author NANCY HOLDER was born in Palo Alto, California. A Navy brat, she went to middle school in Japan. When she was sixteen, she dropped out of high school to become a ballet dancer in Cologne, Germany. An injury at eighteen ended that possible career.

Eventually she returned to California and graduated from the University of California at San Diego with a degree in communications. Soon after, she began to write. Her first sale was a young adult novel with the unfortunate title of *Teach Me to Love*. Thus, she is the Kilgore Trout of the romance world.

Nancy's work has appeared on many bestseller lists. A six-time winner of the Bram Stoker Award, she received a Scribe Award from the International Association of Media Tie-In Writers for Best Novel, and was subsequently named a Grand Master by that organization in 2019. She also received a Young Adult Literature Pioneer Award from RT Booksellers.

She and Debbie Viguié coauthored the *New York Times* bestselling *Wicked* series for Simon and Schuster. They produced many more books together, including the teen thriller *The Rules*. She wrote horror solo and with Melanie Tem for Dell Abyss, and is the author of the young adult horror series *Possessions for Razorbill*. She has sold many projects set in universes such as Teen Wolf, Buffy the Vampire Slayer, Angel, Saving Grace, Hellboy, Smallville, Wishbone, Kolchak the Night Stalker, the Green Hornet, Domino Lady, and Zorro. She novelized the movies *Ghostbusters, Wonder Woman,* and *Crimson Peak*. She has also sold approximately two hundred short stories as well as essays on writing, popular culture and horror.

A Baker Street Irregular, she co-edited *Sherlock Holmes of Baking Street* (with Margie Deck), and has written pastiches, articles, and essays about Holmes for various journals and books. She and Deck are the co-commissioners for an ongoing projected seven-year annotation project of the original manuscript of Sir Arthur Conan Doyle short story, "The Terror of Blue John Gap," for the Arthur Conan Doyle Society.

She is an editor and writer of pulp fiction for *Moonstone*, where she and her writing partner, Alan Philipson, are working on a series of prose stories and comic book/graphic novel series of their creator-owned character, Johnny Fade in Deadtown. A second creator-owned series is underway with another publisher.

She lives in a small town in Washington state with her family, and they are ruled over by a ferocious Corgi named Tater. Find her at her outdated website nancyholder.com, @nancyholder, and facebook.com/holder.nancy.

LIFETIME ACHIEVEMENT AWARD RECIPIENT
KOJI SUZUKI

Koji Suzuki is a Japanese writer who was born in Hamamatsu and lives in Tokyo. Suzuki is the author of the *Ring* novels, which have been adapted into other formats, including films, manga, TV series, and video games. He has written several books on the subject of fatherhood.

VALANCOURT
BOOKS

SPECIALTY PRESS AWARD

The HWA is pleased to present the Specialty Press Award to VALANCOURT BOOKS. The HWA Specialty Press Award is presented periodically to a specialty publisher whose work has substantially contributed to the horror genre, whose publications display general excellence, and whose dealings with writers have been fair and exemplary.

The award was instituted in 1997, largely due to the efforts of long-time HWA member and specialty press aficionado Peter Crowther.

The origins of Valancourt Books date back to 2004, when the press' founders James D. Jenkins and Ryan Cagle had to drive twenty-eight hours to access some rare Gothic horror texts that were only available at one library in the country. With modern publishing technology, they figured there had to be a better way of doing things, and so they started Valancourt Books with the aim of making rare and out-of-print books available to new audiences at reasonable prices.

For its first seven years, Valancourt focused on scholarly editions of 18th and 19th-century texts, from the seven legendary "horrid novels" mentioned in Jane Austen's *Northanger Abbey* to rare Victorian "penny dreadfuls" and late 19th-century popular fiction by authors like Bram Stoker, Marie Corelli, and Richard Marsh. These scholarly editions feature introductions, notes, and contextual materials edited by top scholars from around the world.

More recently Valancourt has moved into more modern horror fiction, rediscovering forgotten mid-century authors like John Blackburn, Gerald Kersh, and Charles Beaumont, as well as some of the lost horror greats of the 1970s and 1980s, like Michael McDowell, Elizabeth Engstrom, Bernard Taylor, and Michael Talbot.

In 2016 Valancourt launched two popular series: *The Valancourt Book of Horror Stories* and *The Valancourt Book of Victorian Christmas Ghost Stories*, and more recently three exciting new series have debuted: *Paperbacks from Hell*, which reprints lost 1970s and 1980s horror novels with their original iconic covers, *Monster, She Wrote*, which spotlights women horror writers, and *Valancourt International*, which publishes horror fiction in translation, including *The Valancourt Book of World Horror Stories*, which was a finalist for the Shirley Jackson Award and World Fantasy Award.

Many of Valancourt's books have been adopted for university courses around the world, several have been filmed or are in production, and many of them have been translated and published throughout the world.

For more information on Valancourt Books and the titles it publishes, please visit our website at www.valancourtbooks.com or find us on Instagram, Facebook, Goodreads, and Twitter.

VALANCOURT
BOOKS

MENTOR OF THE YEAR AWARD

The HWA is pleased to announce the winner of the Mentor of the Year Award: MICHAEL KNOST.

HWA's Mentor Program is available to all members of the organization. This popular program pairs a newer writer with an established professional for an intensive four-month long partnership. For new writers, the Program offers mentees a personal, one-on-one experience with a professional writer, tailor-made to help them grow in their writing and teach them how to better market their work. For experienced writers, the Program allows mentors a chance to pay forward the experience and encouragement other writers gave them when they were starting out. In addition, there is the added benefit of growing as a writer oneself through the act of teaching others. In short, the Program benefits all who participate, regardless of their roles.

Inaugurated in 2014, the Mentor of the Year Award recognizes one mentor in the Mentor Program who has done an outstanding job of helping newer writers. The award is chosen by the current chair of the Mentor Program.

Congratulations to Michael!

"Michael Knost epitomizes what a mentor should be. He is always willing to help writers improve their craft, as both an HWA mentor and outside of the program, as both a teacher and an editor. Writers who have worked with him, or trained under him, universally praise Michael for his honesty, knowledge, and encouragement. This is probably recognition that is long overdue, but Michael's contributions to the HWA, and the horror genre's up-and-coming writers, has always been recognized and appreciated." - J.G. Faherty, HWA Mentorship Program Manager.

MICHAEL KNOST is a Bram Stoker Award®-winning editor and author of science fiction, fantasy, horror, and supernatural thrillers. He has written in various genres and helmed multiple anthologies. He received the Horror Writers Association's Silver Hammer Award in 2015 for his work as the organization's mentorship chair. He also received the prestigious J.U.G. (Just Uncommonly Good) Award from West Virginia Writer's Inc. His *Return of the Mothman* is currently being filmed as a movie adaption. He has taught writing classes and workshops at several colleges, conventions, online, and currently resides in Chapmanville, West Virginia with his wife, daughter, and a zombie goldfish.

THE SILVER HAMMER AWARD

The HWA is pleased to announce the winner of The Silver Hammer Award: KEVIN J. WETMORE, JR.

The HWA periodically gives The Silver Hammer Award to an HWA volunteer who has done a truly massive amount of work for the organization, often unsung and behind the scenes. It was instituted in 1996 and is decided by a vote of HWA's Board of Trustees.

The award is so named because it represents the careful, steady, continuous work of building HWA's "house"—the many institutional systems that keep the organization functioning on a day-to-day basis. The award itself is a chrome-plated hammer with an engraved plaque on the handle. The chrome hammer is also a satisfying allusion to The Beatles' song, "Maxwell's Silver Hammer," a miniature horror story in itself.

Congratulations to Kevin!

KEVIN J. WETMORE, JR. is the author, editor or co-editor of twenty-seven books, including Bram Stoker Award nominees *Uncovering Stranger Things*, *The Streaming of Hill House*, *Devil's Advocates: The Conjuring*, and *Eaters of the Dead: Myths and Realities of Cannibal Monsters*. He is also the author of over a hundred articles and three dozen short stories found in magazines and anthologies such as *Cemetery Dance, Mothership Zeta, Nonbinary Review, Midian Unmade,* and *The Cackle of Cthulhu.* He is the co-chair of HWA's Los Angeles Chapter, has twice co-chaired StokerCon® and served as StokerCon's volunteer coordinator, in addition to serving as curator for the HWA blog Halloween Haunts and chair of the Lifetime Achievement Award committee. In his other life he is a professor of Theatre Arts at Loyola Marymount University where he teaches horror theatre, horror cinema, Japanese theatre, African theatre, Shakespeare, and stage combat.

THE RICHARD LAYMON PRESIDENT'S AWARD

The HWA is pleased to announce the winner of The Richard Laymon President's Award for Service: SUMIKO SAULSON. The Richard Laymon President's Award for Service was instituted in 2001 and is named in honor of Richard Laymon, who died in 2001 while serving as HWA's President. As its name implies, it is given by HWA's sitting President.

The award is presented to a volunteer who has served HWA in an especially exemplary manner and has shown extraordinary dedication to the organization.

Congratulations to Sumiko!

SUMIKO SAULSON (they/them), Social Media Manager for the Horror Writers Association, is an award-winning author of Afrosurrealist and multicultural sci-fi and horror whose latest novel *Happiness and Other Diseases* (book one of the *Metamorphoses of Flynn Keahi*) is available on Mocha Memoirs Press. Other works include the nonfiction title *100+ Black Women in Horror Fiction*, novels *Solitude*, *Warmth*, and *Moon Cried Blood*. Their short stories have appeared in numerous anthologies including *Tales for The Campfire*, *Clockwork Wonderland*, *Tales From the Lake Vol 3*, *Beasts and*

Babes, Scierogenous 2, Colors In Darkness: Forever Vacancy, and *Slay: Tales of the Vampire Noire.* Their poetry has appeared in *Infectious Hope, Siren's Call Magazine,* and *HWA Poetry Showcase VII* and *VIII.* They are the editor of the anthologies *Black Magic Women* (2018), *Scry of Lust* (2019), *Wickedly Abled* (2020) and *Scry of Lust 2* (2021), and the collection *Black Celebration.* They are a comic zine maker and author/illustrator of the graphic novels/comic books *Agrippa* (2013), *Dreamworlds* (2016), and *The Complete Mauskaveli* (2020). They are the illustrator of *Living a Lie* (2015).

Winner of the Afrosurrealist Writers Award (2018), Grand Prize 2017 BCC Voice "Reframing the Other" contest, 2nd Place Carry The Light Sci-fi/Fantasy Award (2016), 2017 Mixy Award, 6th Place in the Next Great Horror Writers Contest (2017). They are the recipient of the 2002 STAND Grant for First Time Directors, 2016 HWA StokerCon® "Scholarship from Hell," 2018 Ara Joe Grant for Zinemakers, 2020 HWA Diversity Grant recipient, and 2021 Ladies in Horror Fiction grant.

Sumiko has an AA in English from Berkeley City College, writes a column called "Writing While Black" for a national Black Newspaper, the *San Francisco BayView,* writes for *Search Magazine,* is the host of the SOMA Leather and LGBT Cultural District's "Erotic Storytelling Hour," and teaches courses at the Speculative Fiction Academy.

THE ANN RADCLIFFE ACADEMIC CONFERENCE:

FIVE YEARS OF FEAR AND LOATHING

by Michele Brittany and Nicholas Diak

Five years of the Ann Radcliffe Academic Conference, what a milestone! The previous four years of AnnRadCon has given a platform to more than eighty-five presentations that furthered horror and gothic scholarship. A substantial amount of these presentations became the precursor to published books and monographs, such as Rahel Sixta Schmitz's *The Supernatural Media Virus: Virus Anxiety in Gothic Fiction Since 1990*, John C. Tibbetts's *The Furies of Marjorie Bowen*, and of course, the entirety of *Horror Literature from Gothic to Post-Modern: Critical Essays*, the Horror Writers Association's first academic publication that contains essays based off presentations from the first two years of AnnRadCon. Since AnnRadCon strives to be a safe space to present scholarship, we have seen many academics returning to the conference to share their work. We could not be more proud of these success stories.

As we enter the second year of the COVID-19 pandemic, the grim reality that the world is a scary place has been solidified. This, of course, is reflected in our pop culture that seeks to either capitalize on or articulate (or both) the pandemic through films, television episodes, books, video games, comics, music, art, and so on. Even pre-pandemic texts now take on new meaning when viewed through a COVID-19 lens (zombie and other contagion films can definitely never be viewed the same way again!).

With the acceptance that the world has been irrevocably changed comes the desire to make sense of it all. One of the primary functions of (horror) academics is to decipher and interpret gothic and horror texts, compose and publish their research, which in turn is consumed not only by other academics, but by fiction authors as well. Scholarly work becomes the research for fiction writers who in turn compose texts which are then analyzed by scholars, ad infinitum. It is a mutually beneficial feedback loop.

This want for academic research was underscored during StokerCon® 2021 when viewership numbers of the virtual AnnRadCon presentations surged by curious convention attendees. This was no doubt due to the easy convenience of AnnRadCon content being available at all hours during the convention via the Hopin platform. Attendees who had not had the opportunity to hear in person scholar presentations before due to scheduling conflicts had the luxury to not only watch the presentations at their leisure, but engage in back and forth dialogue with the presenters via the comments section. This dialogue was critical to both attendee and presenter and it was a pleasure to see it unfold.

As the Ann Radcliffe Academic Conference enters its fifth year of operation, we are pleased to have the best of both worlds: in-person presentations returning as well as online, virtual presentations. This configuration maximizes the accessibility of scholarly content for everyone, and invites even more academics, especially those in other countries impacted adversely by travel restrictions, to take part of the academic track. We hope you will enjoy this year's AnnRadCon presentation offerings and thank you for your support of your fellow academics.

STOKERCON® LIBRARIANS' DAY 2022

by Konrad Stump

After the success of 2021's virtual conference, we've planned an exciting line-up of in-person, hybrid, and virtual programming for StokerCon's 6th annual Librarians' Day. The benefits of this ongoing partnership between the horror and library communities cannot be overstated. In the last few years that relationship, combined with the work of the HWA's Library Committee and the Summer Scares reading initiative, has brought more horror books and authors into libraries than ever before. Libraries now look to the HWA to build their print and digital collections and to connect their communities with the horror genre through public programming.

For those of you new to Librarians' Day, let me share a bit about the array of programming we were able to offer last year, in part because of the advantages of a virtual format. Summer Scares, the HWA's national summer reading initiative, led by a committee of library workers, continued to grow in its third year with Silvia Moreno-Garcia as last year's author spokesperson. We not only expanded our search to international authors, but also, the Summer Scares Programming Guide provided by the Springfield-Greene County (MO) Library returned with programming designed to fit a pandemic, including virtual visits, take-home programming bags, and around-the-town scavenger hunts, as well as an article on programming lessons learned from the pandemic. We saw many libraries across the country take advantage of virtual author visits, and had more library workers reach out to us than ever before, to seek assistance with programming and to share their appreciation of the HWA. Library workers shared their thanks to us for providing easy-to-use resources to expand their collections and engage their patrons during a time when human connection was especially important. We've been able to see readers of all ages discussing horror and its benefits, which is especially encouraging amongst our younger readers, helping them to foster a life-long love of horror.

We were also able to offer three on-demand discussions about the 2021 Summer Scares selections moderated by members of the Summer Scares selection committee, with the Adult panel moderated by Konrad Stump, the YA panel moderated by Becky Spratford, and the Middle Grade panel moderated by Julia Smith. These pre-taped panels debuted at StokerCon® 2021 and were made available on the HWA's YouTube page after the event. Through the YouTube page, you have access to three years' worth of Summer Scares content to not only enjoy yourself, but that you can share with your community. During Librarians' Day itself, we were able to offer these live virtual panels:

The Appeal of a Good Scare: featuring Tim Waggoner, Grady Hendrix, V. Castro, Jessica Guess, John Fram, and Emily Hughes, moderated by Becky Spratford

Thrilling Communities with Chilling Experiences: featuring John Edward Lawson from All Access Con; Alex Giannini from Westport (CT) Library; Evelyn Gathu from Crystal Falls (MI) District Library; and Corey Farrenkopf from Sturgis (MA) Library, moderated by Konrad Stump

Meet the 2020 Diversity Grant Recipients: featuring Jacqueline Dyre, Oghenechovwe Donald Ekpeki, Gabino Iglesias, Nicole Givens Kurtz, Tejaswi Priyadarshi, and Sumiko Saulson, moderated by Linda Addison

Meet the Press: Omnium Gatherum: featuring Lee Murray, Lisa Morton, Kate Maruyama, Donna J.W. Munro, S. Alessandro Martinez, and Kate

Jonez, moderated by Konrad Stump

Totally Bloodless Horror Promotion: featuring Ally Russell, Ladies of the Fright, Adam Cesare, and Cameron Chaney, moderated by Lila Denning

The Scary Truth About Horror Reviews: featuring Emily Vinci for *Library Journal*, Silvia Moreno-Garcia for *The Washington Post*, Gabino Iglesias for NPR and others, and Beth Griffith and Nina James for Night Worms, moderated by Sadie Hartmann.

Nearly five hundred people were able to access Librarians' Day content during StokerCon® 2021 and the week following through extended access, and our pre-recorded Summer Scares panels showed up in the feeds of the HWA's YouTube subscribers.

We are looking forward to seeing you all back in person at Librarians' Day during StokerCon® 2022 on Friday, May 13th in Denver, where we will be offering a fun-filled and informative day of programming designed for library workers, graciously sponsored by LibraryReads and NoveList, with lunch included for one price. And this year, we are also partnering with the Chicagoland HWA Chapter and HWA COS (Colorado Springs) for Librarians' Day to help make your day go more smoothly.

We'll have an exciting slate of in-person programs, including a chance to learn about the 2022 Summer Scares line-up and hear from this year's spokesperson, Alma Katsu. Also appearing in person will be authors Brian Keene, Gabino Iglesias, Lisa Kröger, Daniel Kraus, and more, including a live panel focused on small presses featuring Hailey Piper with Off Limits Press and John Edward Lawson with Raw Dog Screaming Press. You'll also hear from innovative horror program planners who will share how you can adapt their ideas for your community.

As part of our commitment to offer virtual and hybrid content, we will highlight a featured small press with a recorded panel called Meet the Publisher: Off Limits Press. Once again, we will be offering a Meet the Diversity Grant Recipients panel, and we will have a panel on middle grade horror.

All attendees will also receive free books and swag from the authors and publishers who are participating. Anyone who purchased a full StokerCon® ticket is welcome to attend Librarians' Day, with just an add on payment for lunch.

What's so great about Librarians' Day and the Summer Scares reading initiative is that not only do they connect libraries with the horror genre by offering them continuing education and resources, thereby introducing them to new authors, titles, and publishers that they can add to their collections and feature through displays and programming, but also, Librarians' Day and Summer Scares have connected more authors with their local libraries and their local HWA chapters to build a more robust network. So, while you're attending StokerCon®, consider adding Librarians' Day to your schedule, and please explore our virtual content. It is a fantastic networking opportunity for authors to connect with library workers from across the country to start building relationships. Join us for a full day of thrilling discussion and frightful fun as we celebrate our love of horror.

LIBRARIANS' DAY
Horror Writers Association

~~ALONE~~ IN THE DARK:
THE FINAL FRAME FILM FESTIVAL
by Jonathan Lees

We are creatures of habit, content with the personal rituals we perform to conjure a bit of magic in our lives. Strip us of these ceremonies and the savage comes out. As avid horror cinema addicts, we desire the intensity of a communal scream, the relief in a shared bout of nervous laughter, or the shock that reverberates in every seat surrounding us.

We've watched from our living rooms as the studios struggled with new protocols, from daily testing to distanced sets. Our eyes rolled around our skull while swiping through the endless modules of competing streaming networks flooding their platforms and vying for our attention. People who spent years getting a project made saw their work trapped in a perpetual holding pattern. Our favorite theaters kept shuttering their doors, the smell of popcorn long faded from the room.

Art has proven to thrive in times of adversity but what of the truly independent filmmakers, already working on limited resources and stripped-down budgets without the support or finances to carry on like the corporate giants? Within extreme limitations, sometimes our best, most resourceful creations come to light. No one entrenched in the arts or business showcases this better than the short filmmaker. As we gather together once again to revel in the darkest tales told by our current crop of finalists, please applaud this roster of defiant artists who fought to tell their tales despite the odds.

What haunts us now that we have all experienced this shared global panic? What could possibly terrify us beyond entering the public space itself?

Hopefully, as you settle into your seats and the lights go down and the screen comes alive, you find joy in being with one another again. Horror is always at the forefront of infusing our real fears into the bodies of monsters and revealed in the awe-inspiring, unnamable terrors we eagerly expose ourselves to. We willfully march forward to face what most would cower from.

The Final Frame Horror Short Film Competition will present its seventh year of provocative shorts from around the globe, carefully selected to ensure your dreams will be disturbed once more. The pandemic did instruct us well on one note: it is always important to stay connected, no matter what. Offering the program virtually allowed us to stay in touch with everyone who might not have made it to a physical event regardless. This year, as we open the theater doors once again, we will also be offering the competition online, so everyone can scream together no matter where we all are.

Let us rejoin the ritual once again and we'll see you in the dark.

HORROR UNIVERSITY:

AT THE HEART OF STOKERCON AND THE HWA'S MISSION
by James Chambers

The Horror Writers Association's Horror University launched with StokerCon® in 2016. Intended to expand the HWA's mission to help writers to hone their craft, it took inspiration from the horror community tradition of experienced writers taking new writers under their wing to share advice and insight. Different from the the HWA's mentorship program, which fosters a long-term relationship to work toward specific goals, Horror University workshops delve into specific facets of horror writing, such as character development, plotting, writing atmosphere, researching non-fiction, preparing professional manuscripts, and more. It offers opportunities for novice and seasoned writers to explore new avenues of writing, refresh their skills, or learn new techniques. And until 2020, Horror University happened only once a year: at StokerCon®.

COVID-19 shut down almost everything in 2020, including StokerCon® UK and the Horror University session that would've occurred there. In response to the pandemic, the HWA launched the first Horror University Online session in fall 2020. The response—as it had been for the original Horror University—rang overwhelmingly positive. An all-star line-up of instructors—Linda Addison, Jonathan Maberry, Lisa Morton, and Tim

Waggoner—helped make that session a success. So did the many students who signed up for their workshops and took part in them with enthusiasm and dedication. Horror University's first virtual session paved the way for a second online session at StokerCon® 2021, coincidentally the HWA's first fully virtual StokerCon®. With that session, Horror University Online moved to the online platform, Teachable, which also archives recorded workshops for viewing by those unable to attend a live session. After overcoming a few technical glitches, the new format again received a very positive reception.

As a result, Horror University's reach has grown. It has become accessible to HWA members and other writers around the world who are unable to attend StokerCon®. For the first time, the HWA community bridged distances and gaps that previously seemed too wide to span to offer workshops that provide essential building blocks for aspiring authors. As I write this piece for the StokerCon® 2022 Souvenir Book, yet another Horror University Online session has just been announced for early 2022, and we're looking ahead to the first in-person Horror University session in three years at StokerCon® 2022 in Denver, CO. Those new online sessions will be recorded and added to the archive, allowing authors and HWA members—especially fledgling authors entering the horror community in years to come—to tap into the collective experience and knowledge of some of the genre's brightest—and darkest—voices.

Horror University Online and its growing archive supports Horror University's primary goal, which is that students leave their workshops with better insight into the elements and techniques of writing horror, knowledge that they might share in their personal writing community. Many authors participate in small critique groups, local workshops, regional HWA chapters, and other forums beyond StokerCon® and the HWA, which provide opportunities to share what they know. This is the essential philosophy behind the Scholarship from Hell, an annual grant provided by the HWA for one writer to attend StokerCon®, courtesy of the HWA, and attend all (or as many as they choose) of the Horror University workshops. This not only helps the recipient advance their writing but enables them to leverage their StokerCon® and Horror University experience to help their local writing community and the horror community at large. Part of the scholarship application even asks for the applicants' ideas about how they'll do this. It's all part of the HWA's core mission to promote the horror genre, support the interests of horror writers, and provide resources for horror writers to reach their professional goals.

These objectives make Horror University something special. Attending a convention, networking, listening to panel discussions and presentations, finding exciting books in the dealers room all make for a memorable and influential experience. But Horror University provides something these other tracks don't: intensive, hands-on work with talented and accomplished instructors. Now that it has transitioned online, Horror University's reach has grown, and the new archive ensures its legacy will last long after the fleeting moments of a convention end.

As the main coordinator for Horror University at StokerCon® 2018, 2019, 2021, 2022, and the Horror University Online sessions to date, I've experienced many of my most rewarding moments in the HWA working with instructors and students—and even teaching a workshop a couple of times. The instructor and workshop topics change. New and different students sign on each year. The one thing that never changes is the innate curiosity and passion horror writers display for learning and honing their craft—and the generosity the instructors show in sharing their knowledge. Through Horror University and Horror University Online, the HWA continues to support an important part of its mission—supporting authors and promoting the genre. The heart of the horror genre is beating strong these days.

Presented by the **Horror Writers Association**

HWA POETRY SHOWCASE:
THE POINT OF POETRY
by Angela Yuriko-Smith

"What's the point of poetry?"

I was asked this question years ago when I was still unsure if the label of poet fit on me. The answer was too nebulous in my mind to squeeze into a casual reply, so I think I just said something unimpressive like *...um*. Inwardly I was offended and shocked but perhaps the real issue that kept my reply to the monosyllabic was that I was asking myself the very same question.

Like many teens, I spewed out poetry in massive piles of college ruled notebook paper. I was anti-social, dysfunctional and writing was the only thing I felt competent at. Then I discovered Literary Club. I imagined a room full of anti-social, dysfunctional, nerds like myself discussing favorite books and sharing our work. This wasn't the case. After one meeting I stopped writing poetry for the next thirty years.

When I did start writing poetry again, it certainly wasn't because I considered myself a poet. I repeated this to anyone who would listen. Officially, I was trying to get over my fear of public speaking, and I practiced at the local open mic venues.

When I finally published my first chapbook, it wasn't because I was a poet. I helped a friend publish *his* first chapbook and since I'd already done the work to design his, I made my own. "No one will ever even know" I told my husband when I hit *publish*.

That was *In Favor of Pain* back in 2016. It wound up nominated for an Elgin. Not only had my invisible poetry book been noticed, but it also had been *nominated*—exposed! *People are going to think I'm a poet*, I whined to my husband. His answer back: *aren't you?* I didn't know.

This is about the time the question of poetry came up. I spent a month afterwards role playing what I should have said. I began to realize there was a more vital question behind the first one. Was I qualified to even answer his question—*was* I a poet?

Eventually I answered yes to that, but only after a lot of arguments with my internal critic. If I hadn't found such phenomenal support for poetry in the HWA community, I don't think I would have ever admitted it. Peter Salomon not only bought my first poem for the *HWA Poetry Showcase Volume II*, but he also tolerated me stalking him through convention halls so I could ask him about my submission status. I'm positive he didn't remember my poem in that slush pile, but his encouragement (true or not) made the difference for me.

As an awkward, closeted poet I found a solid place to unfold paper wings in the HWA. Friends like Marge Simon and Linda D. Addison helped me develop my voice. My first poetry workshop with Linda blew my mind open as to all that poetry could be. Marge gave me such good insight once, and I wound up reworking an entire chapbook. That experience gave me permission to acknowledge that I was a poet, and qualified to answer that earlier question.

"What's the point of poetry?" This is what I wish I had answered:

There is no "point" to poetry. A point is too small a measurement to encompass such a vast topic. To try and define poetry in this way would be like assessing an iceberg by what is seen on the surface. Approach both poetry and icebergs with caution to avoid coming to pieces. To try and put the purpose of poetry into trim packaging is as tricky as deciding the textbook answer to the meaning of life.

A better question would be *why*. Why do we write poetry?

At its best, poetry is an instrument of power. The first poems were uttered by shamans and witches in the form of spells. Poetry is a way of passing on knowledge in a holistic way, capturing nuance to flavor fact. It's a way to tell an authentic truth while protecting privacy. It inspires revolution. Set to music, it can define a generation. At its simplest it can be a rhyme for children.

Why we write poetry may seem like a grand, esoteric question with a swathe of complicated variables, but I think it distills down into a simple answer all poets—all artists—would agree on: we write poetry because we have poems inside of us. We create because creation is a state of being. Dogs bark, babies cry, and writers write. Like oysters, a grain of an idea lodges and we can't help but transform it into something new.

I was a poet unable to admit it, even to myself. Sadly, there are thousands of negative literary clubs waiting to snuff out the creative lights. That's why organizations like the HWA and their annual *Poetry Showcase* are so important. Rather than tearing down, we build up.

If I'm ever asked that question again, hopefully I wouldn't waste my answer on a conflicted *um*. I'd like to think I would offer an intelligent discourse on how culturally vital poetry is, but I'm sure my answer will wind up being brief so I can get back to my coffee/beer/thoughts/book/friends.

"What's the point of poetry?"

What I should have said: What's the point *without* poetry?

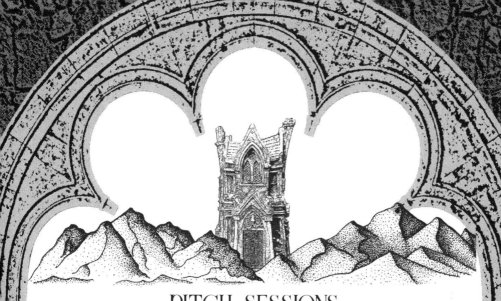

PITCH SESSIONS

by Rena Mason and Brian W. Matthews

Once again, StokerCon® will offer attendees the opportunity to pitch their works directly to publishers, editors, and agents. And once again, it will be in-person!

WHAT IS A PITCH?

A pitch is a concise, engaging description of your project meant to pique the interest of the person to whom you are pitching your story. Make your pitch short—two or three sentences *at most*—and be prepared to answer questions.

WHAT SHOULD I PITCH?

Pitch finished projects. Do not pitch ideas. Make sure your work is error-free and ready to submit. However, do not bring the manuscript with you. If someone shows interest in your work, they will ask you to submit it once you return from StokerCon®.

TO WHOM SHOULD I PITCH?

Choose pitch takers who actually represent your project. If you've written a young adult horror novel, make sure the person/people to whom you want to pitch represent/publish YA horror. This is a critical part of the pitch process—do your homework before you chose your pitch takers. You have one shot with these people. Make sure it counts.

How Do Pitch Sessions Work?

There are a limited number of pitch sessions for each publisher, editor, or agent assigned on a first-come, first-served basis, in the order the requests are received. When you pre-register for a pitch session, list up to three of your preferred pitch takers. This helps your chances to get at least one of your favored choices.

What to Expect at a StokerCon® Pitch Session?

Pitch sessions are scheduled for Saturday, May 14th from Noon to 2 p.m. in the Four Square Ballroom of the Curtis Hotel. Prior to the pitch session, publishers, editors, and agents taking pitches will appear on a panel to discuss the best ways to pitch your project, what they are looking for in a pitch, and what not to do while pitching. Anyone scheduled to give a pitch is strongly advised to attend this panel. Each pitch lasts ten minutes. You will have five minutes to pitch your project, and then an additional five minutes for question-and-answer. At the ten-minute mark, you will be notified your pitch session is over. At that time, smile, thank the person across from you, and exit the ballroom. We typically have over sixty pitch sessions scheduled, and timing is critical. Any holdup throws the whole schedule off. Also, please report to the Four Square Ballroom at least fifteen minutes before your scheduled pitch time to guarantee your place.

What If You Don't Get a Pitch Session with Your Top Choice?

Demand is high for pitch sessions. It's possible you may not get your top choices. Don't despair! Most agents and editors attend the full StokerCon® weekend and are willing to chat with you at other times during the convention—as long as you approach them in a polite, professional manner. Maybe offer to buy them a drink at the bar. But most of all, be considerate, be concise, and don't take up too much of their time.

A LITERARY HISTORY OF DENVER
by Maria Abrams

Katherine Anne Porter described Denver as a "western city founded and built by roaring drunken miners" in her 1939 novella collection: *Pale Horse, Pale Rider*. Fast forward nearly one hundred years later, and Denver is still famous for its alcohol (we have over 150 breweries in the city alone), but less so for its literary presence. Unless, of course, you begin to explore the city and realize the richness of this community.

HISTORY

Arguably, the city's literary forefather is Thomas Hornsby Ferril. A lifelong Denver resident, Ferril not only became Colorado's first poet laureate, but also frequently wrote essays for *The Rocky Mountain Herald*. His Victorian home is still on Downing Street, the same home where Ferril famously hosted writers such as Robert Frost and Dorothy Parker. And anyone who even got to say two words to Dorothy Parker is enviable in my book.

His words, engraved in the Colorado State Capitol, ring true of the city:

"Here is a land where life is written in water...
Look to the green within the mountain cup..."

Born in Denver in 1909, novelist John Fante often wrote highly of Colorado especially after his move to Los Angeles. "I am going home, back to Colorado, back to the best damned town in the USA." Okay, that quote was about Boulder, but I would love to get Fante's thoughts about Denver today. I would be amiss not to mention Fante and not note that his biggest fan was none other than Charles Bukowski, who even referred to Fante as a "god." Talk about major praise.

Other notable Denver residents included Jack Kerouac who lived in Lakewood for a while and famously wrote, "Down in Denver, all I did was die" in a book you might all know: *On The Road*. Annie Proulx also lived in Lower Downtown (or as the locals call it, LoDo) where she commented on her "view of a Ferris wheel and a nutcase on the top floor" in her memoir *Bird Cloud*. Before you ask, no, that nutcase wasn't me. I moved to the city years after that memoir was published in 2011.

BOOKSTORES

If you're like me, you can't pass a bookstore without going inside and buying up half the store. One of the most tempting includes the Tattered Cover. Founded in 1971 as a tiny, one thousand square foot space in Cherry Creek. It quickly grew in popularity and in size. Today, there are five locations in and around Denver, with an upcoming sixth location planned. If you flew into the Denver International Airport, you may have spotted one near each concourse, A, B, and C. The Tattered Cover is the state's largest, independent bookstore. However, it's not the only one worth noting.

BookBar, located on Tennyson Street in the vibrant Berkeley neighborhood, not only sells great books, but also partners with many community endeavors such as Denver Writes, Reading Partners, and the Colorado Coalition for the Homeless. It frequently hosts readings from local and upcoming authors.

In the search for that hard-to-find book? Visit Capitol Hill Books, located on Colfax, a quaint used bookstore in a vibrant neighborhood. At the time of writing this article, the store was hit by a large pick-up truck and is in the process of rebuilding its one hundred-year-old building. So, there's no better time to stop in and show some support by buying a copious number of books. You can thank me later.

COMMUNITY

The largest writer's group in the city is Lighthouse Writers which was founded in 1997 by Michael Henry and his wife Andrea Dupree. Since then, it has moved numerous times, from Curtis Park to Five Points to Thomas Hornsby Ferril's old home on Downing Street, but its mission has stayed the same: "to provide the highest caliber of artistic education, support, and community for writers and readers in the Rocky Mountain Region and beyond."

Founded in 1898, the Denver Women's Press Club continues to be a leading professional membership organization for women in writing. It hosts many networking events as a way for women in the field to cultivate friendships and provide writing support. And personally, I love one of their founding principles, which they still follow today: a haven to drive dull care away.

Looking for a place to soak up some art in a coffee house setting? The Mercury Café is a hip, little joint on California Street that offers daily gatherings full of poetry, dancing, theater, and open mics.

No longer the quiet oasis from the bustling mining towns in the 1800s, Denver is now a lively city where arts and culture run rampant. Voted the United States' eleventh most literate city (edged out by Boston, Portland, and Seattle) by Jack Miller in 2016, Denver's literary scene is only going to become more and more booming.

ABOUT THE AUTHOR

MARIA ABRAMS is a horror writer and graphic designer. She currently lives in Colorado with her rescue pets and one life-size Chucky doll. Find her online on Twitter @AbramsWriter.

A GHOSTLY LINE:

BALANCING BEING A WRITER WITH BEING A PARENT

by Christa Carmen

The clock strikes twelve. There's not a second to waste. The lights in the quiet room have already been doused. A staticky hum careens along in the background like an old-fashioned television set ejecting a poltergeist or a plague of locusts descending on a long-deserted town. I tiptoe from the room and shut the door behind me, as slowly and quietly as if sealing a tomb on a spirit known to wander. When the door is latched, I don't wait. I sprint down the hall without looking back.

My socked feet almost slip on the hardwood, but I grip a passing doorframe and spin myself through it. I'm a woman pursued. Or, perhaps, a woman possessed. I'm exhausted, but I won't look at the daybed no matter how it tempts with feathery pillows and chenille throw blankets. I long for a cup of Darjeeling or Ceylon black, but I don't dare risk the scream of the tea kettle. I walk past candles, tarot cards, and crystals, refusing to light, deal, or palm them. With bone-weariness that would be alarming if it wasn't so familiar, I collapse into a chair and...

...write.

Without break and—to the best of my ability—without distraction, I write while my almost two-and-a-half-year-old daughter sleeps. I write though I'd like to sleep myself. I know from experience that if I were to crawl into bed, the nagging guilt over not writing will make it impossible to nap anyway. I write though I'd like to numb my brain with social media, but I disabled the Facebook, Twitter, and Instagram apps and websites on my phone. I write instead of doing laundry, dishes, cleaning the chicken coop, reading, watching Netflix, showering, or making a snack. For the one-and-a-half to two-and-a-half hours my daughter, Eleanor or, Nell, as we call her, naps (on the weekends) or for the first hour-and-a-half after she's fallen asleep for the night (on weekdays, when I work at a pharmaceutical company during the day), I write instead of doing literally anything else.

This is far from disciplined, though it might sound like it. Rather, it's the result of cause-and-effect, and good, old-fashioned cognitive dissonance. Before I got into the habit of writing while Nell slept, I found that writing, or rather, not writing, was the only thing that could pull me out of being in the moment while spending time with her. There was nothing worse than that feeling: enjoying, on one hand, a whimsical new picture book together while a little voice inside my head growled, "any momentum you had on your novel is gone now," or "I guess you're not going to meet that submission deadline after all."

Several times, I tried my hand at writing while spending time with her... nothing ambitious, a few rough paragraphs here or a new story idea outline there, but all this did was make me feel like a no-good, distracted parent and an even worse, distracted writer. I couldn't reconcile the idea that I was being the best mother I could with the belief—however rigid or irrational—that every hour that passed was a missed opportunity to write. Until, that is, I decided to dedicate the only time I was guaranteed to be apart from my daughter to writing. To free up my headspace and silence that nagging little voice once and for all.

Mercifully, the practice worked. Nell sleeps, I write. Nell is awake, I don't write. I never feel like I should be writing when I'm singing, dancing, playing, building, painting, drawing, walking, or chasing chickens with her, and I never feel like I should be with Nell when I'm editing the latest scene in my historical horror novel or starting a new story for an interesting submission call...because she's sleeping! It seems like an entirely obvious solution now, but it's surprising how many "hacks," or whatever you want to call those practices that allow parents—and writers—some semblance of satisfaction, are vague and imprecise on the first go-round.

And it's still a balance, of course. Like anything worthwhile. Some days I absolutely *have* to do the laundry or clean the chicken coop, or my husband stays home while our daughter naps and I meet a friend for a much-needed social interaction over lunch. Some days I'm mentally exhausted, and I consider daydreaming about how to solve the plot snag I've hit while watching the birds (I'm looking at *you*, COVID-purchased suet feeders!) to constitute writing. Some days reading or watching Netflix feels like laziness, but I know it's allowing my brain to rest in the same way my daughter's nap is allowing her to cement the words and concepts she heard me read to her over the course of the day into knowledge and language and memories. But most days, I take the disappointment (maybe even disgust?) I know I'll feel if I squander the time while Nell's sleeping, and use it to fuel my motivation to write. The delight I experience when I spend all afternoon with her having already logged fifteen hundred words is unparalleled. Worth the weight of an ever-growing manuscript in gold.

Writers with children walk a ghostly line, but that line isn't perilous, ethereal, and mysterious because it's so thin and hard to perceive; it's ghostly because we allow it to infiltrate our heads and spin itself into our thoughts, tricking us into believing we're doing something wrong. Balancing that line is an act of fearlessness on par with any horror novel hero or slasher final girl. The trick, so much as I've been able to garner, is to keep the villain, ghost, or ghoul out of your own head.

And maybe there is an element of discipline to balancing things as I do, but writing is discipline in and of itself. Discernment with one's time as much as with characters and commas, clarity and craft. In the end, though, writing brings me joy. If not as much joy as reading to, or watching the birds with, my daughter, then a healthy second. And nothing banishes a ghost more quickly than consistent, unadulterated joy.

ABOUT THE AUTHOR

CHRISTA CARMEN's work has been featured in *Nightmare Magazine, Vastarien: A Literary Journal, Fireside Fiction, Year's Best Hardcore Horror,* and the Bram Stoker-nominated *Not All Monsters: A Strangehouse Anthology by Women of Horror* and *The Streaming of Hill House: Essays on the Haunting Netflix Adaption,* among other publications. Her debut collection, *Something Borrowed, Something Blood-Soaked,* won the 2018 Indie Horror Book Award for Best Debut Collection. Christa holds an MFA in Popular Fiction from Stonecoast, of the University of Southern Maine.

When she's not writing, she keeps chickens, uses a ouija board to ghost-hug her dear departed beagle, and reads books like *Mary Who Wrote Frankenstein* and *The Gashlycrumb Tinies* to her daughter. Most of her work comes from gazing upon the ghosts of the past or else into the dark corners of nature, those places where whorls of bark become owl eyes and deer step through tunnels of hanging leaves and creeping briers only to disappear.

THE VILLAGE THROUGH THE SIDE
OF THE HORROR HOUSE

by Rhonda Jackson Garcia (aka R.J. Joseph)

I always imagined a welcoming party inside the huge, beautiful Horror House I've been obsessed with since childhood. I spent years and years sitting in the front yard, watching the words that were borne from the abode, smiling at the figures I saw in the windows and relishing in the stories they told. First, they wore old-fashioned clothing and were mostly men. As time progressed, few women joined the figures. None who looked like me, though.

One day, I saw a woman with a beautiful afro knock on the big doors. Exquisite words emanated from her being and I wanted more of them. I just knew she'd be embraced and allowed into the house, so she could keep spinning the delightful, decadent stories she had filling her spirit. The door remained closed.

I was confused because I thought Horror House would benefit from her being there, from having her stories filling The Universe around the house and feeding the souls that needed her experiences. She knocked again, and the door opened a sliver. Her enormous talent couldn't be denied and yet she had to slip in through the crack before the door shut resoundingly behind her.

But she was in there. And that was good enough for me.

I bruised and bloodied my knuckles relentlessly for years, trying to gain my own entry through those ornate double doors at the front of the horror writing world, with my knocks going unanswered. I tried the back door, writing and submitting my work to all the heavy hitters and awards committees in the industry, wanting a validity for my experiences and my writing that never came. I continued sitting in the yard outside those doors and watched as numerous stories and films that were homogenous, non-original, and added nothing to the writing canon were published, lauded, paid, and produced.

As mediocre creator after mediocre creator trampled over those of us in the yard to get to the doors that were always open to them—oh, I was never alone in my longing to enter the Horror House; there were quite a few of us at any given time--I noticed a side window to that world. It was covered in bushes, almost hidden. I dragged myself up and went over to peek in. That side window was, indeed, open. I contemplated climbing up through it, but my confidence had been shattered. I thought it would close on me, the glass splintering and slicing me, adding to the other wounds I already had from trying to break through.

Then, an amazing thing happened. Other marginalized horror writers who were already inside that room held the window up, in an open position, with a crack exactly big enough for me and my work to fit through. They didn't try to close the window on me. They didn't yell to the front of the house that I had made my way in, to wait for someone With Authority to come and throw me out.

They helped me climb up and up and embraced me. I recognized many of them, as the community was small, even though it was comprised of many groups. We were different yet we were the same: we all had stories to tell that hadn't been given a wide enough platform. And we had to help each other to get where we all needed to be. Progress would never be made with us fighting among us. We needed solidarity. We had to have our own backs because we cared the most about our successes and had the most to lose in continued defeat and erasure.

The space I entered is one I enjoy occupying. We are a village, one I couldn't function without. The independent, fringe room in the publishing world was designed for me and numerous other marginalized writers who had been kept outside the world behind the big doors of Horror House. Once we all piled up in that room, it started to expand and now it's one of the biggest rooms in the house, sustaining the publishing world when the rest of the domicile is starting to crumble slightly from the weight of perpetually supporting inequity.

We can help stall that decay if more of us are allowed into those other rooms. Until then, we will continue to build and expand the room where we're thriving.

And I am thriving here, in my village. I had to learn my path might not be the one that was most visible. My opportunities lay off the well-worn path up front. The chances I'd been fighting to get presented themselves in abundance once I embraced leaning into the space I'm supposed to occupy. This space, this village, is where I am able to pay the kindnesses shown to me by other writers forward to others.

I promote the work of other marginalized writers. I'm the Lady Behind the Screen, upholding my horror writing siblings when they need a listening ear, or help with promoting their work. I don't shout out their concerns in the public sphere, looking for accolades for lending a helping hand. That's not what a village does to its members. I'm a first reader, a reviewer, and editor, and an opportunity shouter. I'm a panel member, committee worker, charity anthology participant...whatever I'm needed to do. I work hard to take up the mantle of community and support that are the main reasons I am where I am and why I can do what I do.

I will remain here, a steadfast member of the Side of the Horror House Village, because I understand this is where I'm supposed to be. My path within writing and publishing was predetermined by The Universe before I was even born. The road to that destiny has hardly been smooth. This world is difficult to navigate. Fraught with rejections, gatekeepers, and prejudices, it's not a walk for the weak willed.

Through the strength bestowed on me through my village, I've worked tirelessly to advance equity for marginalized writers, though we often see publishing fall short and double down on keeping diverse voices out of range for lucrative opportunities that would enhance our genre and give our readers the quality, inclusive stories they deserve.

There's even more fortitude in numbers and solidarity and my horror writing village and I will continue to work breaking down the walls inside Horror House and in the world outside. We will continue helping each other because we got us.

ABOUT THE AUTHOR

RHONDA JACKSON GARCIA, aka R.J. Joseph, is a Stoker Award® nominated, Texas-based academic and creative writer/professor whose writing regularly focuses on the intersections of gender and race in the horror genre and popular culture. She has had works published in various applauded venues, including the 2020 Halloween issue of *Southwest Review* and *The Streaming of Hill House: Essays on the Haunting Netflix Series.* Rhonda is also an instructor at the Speculative Fiction Academy.

IF YOU GIVE A BOOKSTORE
A HORROR SECTION

by Sadie Hartmann

What an honor it is to be asked to write for this StokerCon® Souvenir booklet you now hold in your hands. I am delighted to have this opportunity to share my love for horror fiction in a general, big picture sense but also in a very specific, "this present moment" way too.

My love of horror was a tiny mustard seed of interest prompting me to steal *Salem's Lot* from my mom's bookshelves and read it in the privacy of my bedroom after bedtime. This tiny seed germinated into passion; matured into a full-blown obsession.

About five years ago I made a dedicated bookish account on Instagram. Due to the overwhelming influence of social media, I began noticing that horror fiction has so much more to offer than what I was finding in bookstores (we'll circle back to this). That's what happens when you have a community of like-minded people in one place from all over the globe. It mimics a swarm of worker bees on a collective mission—FIND THE HORROR! Buzzz Buzzz!

And what did I discover?

Indie. Horror. Fiction.

I don't know how to best communicate the importance of discovering independently published horror fiction, but I can say that finding it was a game changer for me. It has literally changed my life and opened doors for me that ultimately led me down the path to my current career.

Back to bookstores.

Before "bookish social media," I found my horror books in stores and libraries or what I used to call the "K Section" (King-Koontz). Pretty limited selection. Once I became active in a bookish community, my eyes were opened to a whole new world. One day I saw someone recommending an Ania Ahlborn book called, *Brother*, calling it the scariest book they ever read.

Well, I need that. I always need that.

So, I found it, read it, and then bought four more books by Ania Ahlborn. How did I live my best horror-loving life before Ania Ahlborn?

The first book I ever requested in exchange for a review was *Beneath* by Kristi DeMeester. I emailed the powers that be at Word Horde (Ross!) and he took a chance on me; sent me a few titles if I remember correctly back in September 2017. This was a pivotal moment in "Mother Horror" history. I built a symbolic tower of rocks to mark that fall as the "no looking back" season of reading and reviewing horror.

The amazing thing is that horror made its own tower too. Right there in 2017. The upwards trajectory of horror fiction, both indie and traditional and everything that falls adjacent, looks like a hockey stick. The year 2017 saw book releases like, *Kill Creek* by Scott Thomas, *In the Valley of the Sun* by Andy Davidson, *Mapping the Interior* by Stephen Graham Jones, *The Grip of It* by Jac Jemc, *The Devil Crept In* by Ania Ahlborn, *The Changeling* by Victor LaValle, *Her Body and Other Parties* by Carmen Maria Machado and many, many, more.

I don't know if it was because I only just started paying attention, or if horror actually stood up and decided it was time to get noticed. Was it in tandem with indie movie production companies releasing *Big Buzz* films? 2017 was the year of *Get Out* from Jordan Peele, *The Killing of a Sacred Deer*, *The Endless*, *Super Dark Times,* and *The Shape of Water* which is like horror/romance and was a big deal at the Oscars—the horror community claims Guillermo del Toro and Daniel Kraus as our own.

It's no coincidence readers started noticing big box bookstores like Barnes & Noble adding a proper horror section.

HORROR IS IN DEMAND AND WHERE WILL IT ALL GO??

You're going to mix it all in with General Fiction and stock the one hundred copies of the latest Grady Hendrix or Alma Katsu needed to keep up with sales?

Josh Malerman releases like a book every month, when would be a good time to have a dedicated horror section in your bookstore? Just in time to accommodate the sequel to *My Heart Is a Chainsaw* by Stephen Graham Jones or maybe when it's a full-blown trilogy?

Well, too late!!

And maybe when you give a bookstore a horror section, you're going to need some end caps for the overflow. And if you fill up the end caps, you're going to need some extra display tables, especially at Halloween. And don't forget the TikTok accounts who won't stop talking about the last book that

-disturbed them the most

-gave them nightmares

-made them throw their book across the room

because their followers want to have that experience too. To accommodate #booktok trends, bookstores now have a whole separate table for recommendations coming in from that platform. Horror is here to stay! It's making big waves and winning all the literary awards. Horror movies are getting nominated and going home with the top prize. *Parasite*, 2020's Oscar winner is a horror movie—anyone who says otherwise maybe has COVID brain?

My bottom line here is, we're living in a global pandemic. A global warming crisis. A nation divided. We're living in a state of unrest and horror. It's only natural readers want to escape into something more fucked up than our own lives. Horror fiction is on the rise and filling that endless void in our souls created by anxiety and worry and LOCKDOWN. I couldn't be more proud. It's a great time to be a horror fan.

ABOUT THE AUTHOR

SADIE HARTMANN aka Mother Horror reviews horror for *Cemetery Dance* and *SCREAM Magazine*. She is the co-owner of the horror fiction subscription company, Night Worms. She lives in Tacoma, WA with her husband of 20+ years where they enjoy perfect weather, street tacos, and hanging out with their three kids. They have a Frenchie named Owen.

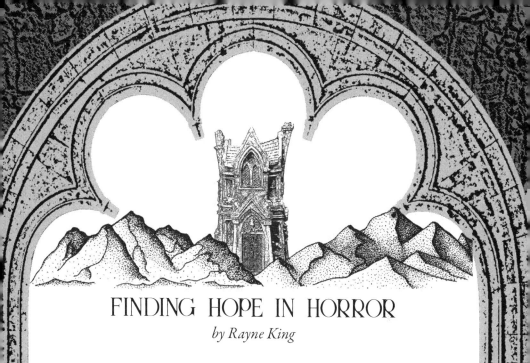

FINDING HOPE IN HORROR

by Rayne King

Horror is subjective by nature, but in 2020 we faced a universal horror in the form of a global pandemic. COVID-19 upturned our lives virtually overnight, casting us into a nightmarish reality that bordered on apocalyptic. Highly contagious and possibly fatal, COVID-19 compelled state governments to enforce lockdown protocols in an attempt to flatten the curve of the virus. As my home state shut down, a list of essential jobs was announced. Working in the logistics business, my place of employment qualified, and I was deemed an essential employee.

The passing scenery during my commutes turned unfamiliar. The interiors of department stores were vacant and unlit. Roads were void of regular traffic. Medical tents popped up in the desolate parking lot of a bygone corporation, acting as makeshift testing sites for the virus. National Guard vehicles were spotted, driving around as if patrolling. Fear and uncertainty hung in the air, thick like black smoke. It felt like driving through a ghost town. Contrary to this, business boomed in the shipping industry due to a monumental surge in online shopping.

The stress caused by an increased workload and the constant worrying over contracting the virus pushed me to a breaking point. In what some may view as an ironic twist to combat the anxiety that plagued me, I leaned on my love of horror to help cope during such unprecedented times. As a lifelong horror aficionado, the genre had always been a source of comfort for me whenever I was distressed. Cozying up with a horror book or film was a way for me to decompress.

I discovered the horror community around this time completely by accident. I'd been scouring the internet for new horror books to read, which led me to find a group of like-minded individuals. Members within the horror community were friendly and welcoming, and I felt an instant connection with them as if we were all kindred spirits. Discussions focused on the genre were lively and insightful. Socializing in the traditional sense had ceased to exist in order to limit possible exposure to the virus, and these conversations eased the feeling of isolation.

Corresponding with writers within the horror community rekindled a fire in me, and soon I wanted to write a piece of fiction with the intention of sharing it. As an avid reader, ideas for my own stories had sprouted up over the years, but never anything concrete. Every time I tried my hand at writing, I found the results to be underwhelming. Nothing more than bits of fiction journalistic in style that were for my eyes only. Having no guidance, my interest waned over the years, and I gradually stopped altogether. But speaking to writers at various stages of their careers encouraged me to give it another stab. I began working on what would become my debut novella. Seeing writers in the community share information regarding their own works in progress inspired me to do the same. The enthusiasm and positivity my contributions were met with helped keep me motivated. It was a communal experience, swapping updates on how our respective projects were going. Through trial and error, I completed my novella. It was a baptism by fire, since I was learning how to construct a narrative as I went. It was finished, though, and I had the support from the horror community to largely thank for that.

Content with my manuscript, I shelved it until I could figure out how to proceed from there. Time passed, and the holiday season was upon us. Work grew busy again. The flu season was in full swing, adding another layer of uncertainty to the pandemic. A renewed sense of vulnerability prevented me from concentrating on anything other than endurance. Creative writing and activity within the horror community dwindled as I shifted my focus to staying healthy, both physically and mentally. I felt disheartened and lacked the stimulation I'd grown accustomed to. Restless and morose, I grinded through long shifts at work until a gloomy holiday season passed, where the virus prevented us from spending time with family and friends.

Work eventually quieted down, and I eagerly reacquainted myself with the horror community. The spirited interactions picked up right where they left off, and it felt like returning home after being away. Resolving to get my novella in the hands of readers quickly, I decided to go the self-publishing route. Members of the community who were well rehearsed in this process pointed me in the right direction. They steered me toward cover artists, editors, and formatters. Their assistance made the process incredibly efficient, and before long my debut was ready.

Having my book out in the wild further established my connections within the community. In a surreal experience, people I'd grown to greatly admire read it and shared their thoughts. Others reached out to me to discuss it. As a new writer on the scene, it was humbling to see all these people give my book a chance, and I was profoundly grateful for their selflessness. Not only did the horror community provide me with an escape from the horrors of the outside world during a difficult year, but the kindness displayed by its members filled me with immense hope.

And I do my best now to pay it forward by lending a helping hand to whoever needs one.

Because that is what a community does.

We bring each other up.

ABOUT THE AUTHOR

Rayne King is an author of horror fiction, with several short stories and the novella, *The Creek*, to his name. As an autodidact, he has learned to write through trial and tribulation. His influences are widespread, ranging from magical realism to cosmic horror. Because of this, his writing borrows elements from a multitude of genres, as he feels comfortable using whatever tools necessary to tell his dark tales. He lives in the Hudson Valley with his family. Find him on Twitter via @Channel_King.

A LITTLE LESS HAUNTED THAN BEFORE

by Eric LaRocca

When my dear friend, Cynthia Pelayo, first contacted me to write a brief essay reflecting on my experience throughout the past year as I've come to find a home in the horror community, I found myself filled with a profound sense of joy—an indescribable feeling of camaraderie and kinship with kindhearted individuals near and far. It's quite safe to say that we are currently living through a traumatic historical event with the presence of COVID-19 in our world. Despite the trials and tribulations we've collectively faced, humanity continues to showcase its admirable resilience—the very human need to survive, the all too humanistic urge to thrive. As I reflect on the year of 2021, I realize that I've witnessed the most disgraceful aspects of humanity as well as the most exemplary and outstanding examples of us as a human race.

I certainly was never prepared for the outrageous success of my novella, *Things Have Gotten Worse Since We Last Spoke*, and I often found myself struggling to cope with the catastrophe of triumph—the all-consuming misfortune that typically accompanies the arrival of acclaim or notoriety. It was during the few months after the novella's successful release that I quickly discovered who had my best interest at heart and who did not. Those who I had once considered dear friends splintered away and exhibited contempt or, even worse, jealousy. I found my community growing smaller and smaller until I was surrounded by a tight knit group of writers, artists, creators who appreciated my work and wanted to see me succeed just as much as I wanted to see their victory as well.

I suppose my most meaningful takeaway from the past year or so and finding a modicum of success in the horror community has had me realize that the size of one's circle is unimportant. It's all about the quality of the folks with whom you associate. My circle has become smaller and smaller over the years and, at first, I thought perhaps that was a problem or an issue I needed to remedy. I now realize that there's no such issue. It's an honor to engage in a small circle of talented and like-minded writers.

Moreover, what has sustained me throughout the pandemic and the bouts of imposter syndrome that creep into my mind at the most inopportune of moments has been when giant pillars of the online horror community have reached out to me and shared how much they genuinely enjoyed my work. I've had the distinct privilege of interacting with countless icons of horror over the past twelve months—gifted writers and skilled creators who I'm quite surprised even know of my trivial existence. Interacting with these giants and feeding from their wisdom has been a balm unlike any other. Of course, I would love to share with you the names of some of the people who have reached out since the launch of *Things Have Gotten Worse Since We Last Spoke*, but to publicly name them would be embarrassing for me and I prefer to keep those conversations as private and as guarded as much as possible because they are so meaningful to me.

Bearing that in mind, as I move forward toward a new year with new projects and new friends, I would be honored to take this opportunity to thank everyone in the horror community for their kindness, their generosity, their unwavering support. I must confess, I've felt haunted, burdened, monstrous for most of my life, but being welcomed so enthusiastically, so unabashedly by this community has shown me a love unlike any I've ever received.

Because of you, dear reader, I feel a little less haunted than before.

ABOUT THE AUTHOR

ERIC LAROCCA (he/they) is the author of *Things Have Gotten Worse Since We Last Spoke* and *The Strange Thing We Become and Other Dark Tales*. He is an active member of the Horror Writers Association and currently resides in New England with his partner. For more information, please follow @ejlarocca on Twitter or visit ericlarocca.com.

WHY HORROR IS MY HOME

by Janine Pipe

I am passionate about horror. Whether books, movies or books about movies, I love all things spooky and scary, gory and gnarly. It is where I feel at home. And the people within the horror community, my fellow writers, creators, readers, are the people I feel most comfortable among. When the pandemic first hit, we couldn't see our real-life friends and colleagues. We couldn't drive to see family. We were housebound. Everything was conducted online, over a phone or on a screen. Therefore, the fact that total strangers lurking behind an avatar should become so important isn't really that strange.

And thank goodness for those Tweeters, those people whose names I knew from Amazon pages and my bookshelves, who I never thought for a moment would accept little old me into their gang. But they did. Not only did they accept me, they *welcomed* me. I had little to offer or give back but what I could do, and continue to do always, is support them. Organically through the importance of ensuring I gave something back, my genuine enthusiasm and excitement shone through. My eagerness to learn, my constant cheerleading and encouragement of others became apparent. People wanted me on board with their projects, wanted my advice on how to promote things and how to be so positive. They were suddenly looking to me for guidance.

When I received my first acceptance for a short story from Kandisha Press, I wanted to bottle that feeling and never let it go. That incredulity that someone believed in me, that someone enjoyed my voice and storytelling. I wanted to repeat that sensation again over and over but also, I wanted to help others achieve it. I have always been a believer in karma and the adage of 'paying it forward' and I knew this would be my ethos within the world of writing. I might still be near the beginning of my journey, but I share whatever lessons I've learned, good and bad, along the way. I was lucky enough to have several unofficial mentors, people who has been doing this for a long time and had many helpful tips and warnings. In turn I pass them along to others rising up the ranks looking for exposure or support or a way to secure that first elusive acceptance.

The natural progression was to start putting things together myself. Without the fiscal backing or technical knowledge and experience, I knew I couldn't just open up a press and start pretending I knew how to put something together. Honesty along with loyalty is one of my most important qualities, a litmus test of sorts. So, I approached Jill Girardi at Kandisha Press (circling back to that first acceptance, remember?) about an all women slasher/women who kill anthology and Leza Cantoral and Christoph Paul at Clash Books about a horror based coming-of-age anthology with an Amblin-esque nostalgic twist. I proposed taking the lead as editor/curator but allowing them to use their expertise and stellar reputation to assist, guide and put me in my place where needed. Somehow this has led to one amazing, completed anthology, SLASH-HER (Kandisha Press), and one very exciting open call for NOWHERE FAST (Clash Books) with some absolutely stellar names attached. It showed me that these things can be achievable if you put your mind to it and your heart in it.

But, it takes a village. And in every successful village, there is a support system. In every successful leadership, there is an entourage of people. We need each other. This doesn't mean we have to force ourselves to like everything each other does, quite the opposite. We all have different tastes and opinions. But what is important is the support. I have learnt I can share someone's art, recognise the hard work that has gone into it even though it is not my cup of tea. And if I know other people who do enjoy that brand, I will be sure to recommend it to them. That's support. It should be real and honest but positive.

Thank those who support you, remember them, return the favor. Be the person who others aspire to not because of so-called talent, but because of your positive attitude. Prove you are loyal, demonstrate you can be trusted. Never ever break that. People will forgive many indiscretions, but not betrayal.

And that lookout has led me to where I am today. A Boss Babe as my good friend Sadie Hartmann, aka Mother Horror and co-owner of the phenomenal subscription service Night Worms, jokingly refers to us. Someone who came from nowhere but showed a passion. Someone who is able to rally the troops when needed and connect people. Someone who has proved themselves to be a hard worker, passionate and keen to learn. And someone who is not afraid to reach for the stars. Maybe I am lucky. As well as karma, I am a believer in serendipity and sometimes just being in the right place at the right time with the right person opens the door you need.

As I look back at all I have achieved, I am proud. I am humbled by the number of things I've been invited to, honored to have been a part of. A huge part of that is networking. Follow people, interact, don't be afraid to tell them that you love their work. Authors, editors, publishers, directors, actors. Any type of creator loves to be told someone has enjoyed their work. It isn't arse-kissing. It isn't sucking up to tell someone you admire them, that THEY inspire you. But share that love with everyone. Don't be afraid to tell the celebs but also tell that indie author, that aspiring writer who trusted you to beta read their submission.

It has not all been plain sailing though. Although I choose not to air my dirty washing online, there have been plenty of knocks to my confidence on this journey. It is true that to succeed in this business you need a thick skin. This is usually in reference to reviews as no matter what you produce you can not and will not please everyone. You need to know that and roll with it. But it can be more dismaying and confusing when it is other members of the community. Just try not to take things personally.

That may sound easy for me to say but it is something I truly and strongly believe now more than ever.

Horror is home. It means different things for different people but for me, it is where I am comfortable. It's where my excitement and passion can shine through. It's where I can read books and say OMG I LOVED THAT! It's where I can watch movies and say OMG I want to do that! And it's where I can meet and talk to people who love it just as much as I do. I have made friends. I have made colleagues. But I have also made family. I have people who love and support me. I have homes to visit all over the world. Horror has my heart. And I couldn't be happier.

ABOUT THE AUTHOR

Trading in a police badge and then classroom, JANINE PIPE is a full-time Splatterpunk Award-nominated writer, whilst also being a mum, wife and Disney addict. Influenced by the works of King from a young age, she likes to shock readers with violence and scare them with monsters—both mythical and man-made. When she's not killing people off, she likes to chew the fat with other authors—reviewing books and conducting interviews for *Scream Magazine, Cemetery Dance,* and *Horror DNA*. You'll likely find her devouring work by Glenn Rolfe or watching Neil Marshall movies. Her biggest fans are her loving husband and daughter. One day she will write that screenplay she keeps waffling about. Follow her on Twitter @janinepipe28.

GOING WITHIN
by Mary Rajotte

We all make homes for ourselves in the world. Places to hide from trouble. Where we build ourselves anew. Places that inspire us to delve deep, to hone our imaginations so we can face the trials and tribulations that challenge us. When the pandemic hit and severed our ties to that sanctuary we'd created together—that haven of collective belonging, where even in the gathering darkness, we found kinship that carried us through shadow—it was a loss that made us all feel vulnerable; myself included.

Cancerian by nature, born under the sign of the crab, my home has always been my sanctuary. But even after retreating to that usual place of safety, something was different about it. Even with its ambience—incense cones for solace, candles for comfort, moonstones for magic—the shadows not only found a way to seep in, but they felt more treacherous than before. Those friends I relied on to help me stave off the peril lurking just out of sight had their own terrors to face. The only way for me to keep my space safe was to burrow deeper, to get lost in the wonderment of writing again, and to find that place within myself where I could create far from the uncertainty of the world outside.

It was only when I had the time to look inward that I found I'd been neglecting that gift. Allowing self-doubt and competitiveness, and maybe even a bit of my Cancerian nature to take control. Moody? Who, me?

Stubborn? Bite your tongue! But it was vital, this place where I went to ignite my imagination away from the turmoil that had made writing feel frivolous in the wake of everything going on outside.

Instead of giving in to those shadowed thoughts, I found that seed of my creative spirit, nestled deep and longing to be nurtured. I fell back in love with the artistic process, dedicating time to my craft. I worked hard, trying not to focus on the abundance of my output and instead, to the caliber of my words. And in all that experimentation, I became reacquainted with myself, reigniting that inventiveness within me, one mired under hesitancy for far too long. But as much as I was being my usual Crab self, thriving in the protective bubble I'd conjured, that longing to share my creations with others was fierce.

But back in the outside world, our collective home sat shuttered. Our connections were now digital, vital to that feeling of belonging but without the closeness. That desire to sit near, to tell stories across the table, to feed off one another's energy was still there, maybe more fiercely now than it had ever been.

So, I built a new place. A netherworld of creative minds. A space, even if only digital, that gave us the courage to whisper new tales. A place rich in the music of laughter and chatter. One where we understood the struggles. Where we commiserated the things we'd lost and cheered each other on. We persevered together. And in doing so, it gave us that sense of home that only comes with the connection to one's kindred spirits. A place that not only nurtures that artistic spark, but ignites it.

And my friends in this place helped me to thrive. 2021 was my most successful and prolific year of my career. I wrote more than I ever have before. I challenged myself. Took more chances. I sent out more stories and received more acceptances than any other year since I started writing.

Was it the magic I created in that cozy little nook? The devotion to finding my voice again? The freedom to explore, to unabashedly reignite my love affair with writing? Or the connections to others, not as physically close as before, but stronger somehow, that helped me conjure that magic?

The places we make our own are just as important to the soul as they are to our need for comfort. And whether near or far-flung, whether digital or in-person, these spaces where we ponder and invoke the muses, where we evoke and dream, are crucial. No matter how many obstacles we face, no matter the distance between us, we all have that place inside ourselves. At first, to create, then, to share, a space that's familiar, comforting, one that, when the time comes, we can open it up to those kindred spirits and together again at last, mingle in our shared magic.

ABOUT THE AUTHOR

Canadian author MARY RAJOTTE has a penchant for penning nightmarish tales of folk horror and paranormal suspense. Her work has been published in a number of anthologies, including *In Somnio: A Collection of Modern Gothic Horror Fiction* (Tenebrous Press), *Autumn Noir* (Unsettling Reads) and *Gothic Blue Book VI: A Krampus Carol* (Burial Day Books). She is currently compiling her first collection and querying her first novel. Sometimes camera-elusive but always coffee-fueled, you can find Mary at her website www.maryrajotte.com or support her Patreon for exclusive fiction at www.patreon.com/maryrajotte

WRITING DURING DIFFICULT TIMES
by Tim Waggoner

Writing isn't always easy at the best of times, and I think you'll agree with me that what the world has been going through with COVID doesn't even come close to the best of times. Most of us have day jobs or, if we're full-time freelancers, we cobble together a living from different types of writing and writing-adjacent activities. We're used to having to squeeze in our creative writing when we can, and we give it what energy we can muster.

But writing is even harder during times of great stress. A pandemic—with its health and economic effects—is obviously one of these times. But are there are more than enough personal stresses that we must confront in our lives. Illnesses, divorces, troubles at work, problems with our children, difficulty paying bills... It's not a stretch to say we're always dealing with stress of one kind or another in life, and while some creative people may thrive in the midst of stress, many of us—maybe most—find stress to be a creativity-killer.

So if you're having trouble writing during the pandemic (or any other stressful time in your life), here are some ideas that might help you get the words flowing again.

- Don't tell yourself you have to produce a specific amount. If you decide you should write five pages a day, every day, and you don't make this quota, you'll feel like a failure and get down on yourself. Mental and creative energy is hard to sustain during extended stressful periods. If you write ten pages one day, two pages the next, and none for the next five days, that's okay.

- Write when you can. You might not be able to follow a set schedule for one reason or another. If that's the case, fit writing in when you can. Try to write *something* between the time you wake up in the morning and the time you go to sleep for the night. However much it is, whenever you produce it, if you get it done before your head hits the pillow, that's all that matters.

- Write in short bits of time throughout the day. If you find it hard to concentrate for any length of time, write for five or ten minutes, then go do something else. Come back later and do another five or ten. Repeat this as many times during the day as you can manage. You can also set yourself a schedule: write ten minutes every hour (or every two hours or three hours). Set an alarm to help remind you.

- Write small stuff. Write flash fiction or poems. Write one paragraph, one sentence. Writing small can not only relieve the pressure to produce a lot of work in one session, it's easier when you can only concentrate for short periods as well.

- Write something that's not for publication. Forget the markets. Write something for the sake of writing it. Write something that's just for you. Write something fun. Maybe it'll turn out to be something you'll polish and submit to a market later, maybe not. All that matters is that you're feeding your creative self.

- Write for (and maybe with) your family and friends. Connecting to our loves ones during difficult times can make all the difference in how we get through those times. If you have kids and they're home all day, write a story for them. Write a play for them to act out. Write stuff with them. Collaborate on a story with a friend. Do a round-robin story with a group of friends.

- Keep a journal. If all you can focus on is the pandemic, then write about it. Write about your thoughts, fears, hopes... If this is all you write, that's okay. You're still writing. But if you get your feelings out in your journal—especially if you write it earlier in the day— you might clear enough mental and emotional space in your head to compose your creative work later.

- Write to your new biorhythm. If your daily schedule has changed, your biorhythm might have too. Maybe you used to write at night before bed, but now you can't. Try writing first thing in the morning. Or if mornings used to work for you, try nights. When do you feel you have the least stress during the day? Try writing then.

- Try something new. The old saying "A change is as good as rest" applies here. If you normally write fantasy, try writing mystery. If you normally write fiction, try nonfiction or poetry. Write song lyrics. Write a script. The novelty of trying something new might give you fresh creative energy. And don't worry about how good or publishable this new stuff might be. Just write it. Use it as therapy. Have fun with it. Learn from it.

- Write outside. I'm not big outdoor person, but my wife is. She needs to be outside every day, even if she just goes into our backyard and putters in the garden. If you find yourself getting depressed staying indoors because of the pandemic (and unable to write), maybe you should try writing outside and see if that helps. If nothing else, it'll probably be good for your soul.

Whatever you do, don't put pressure on yourself to be anything than other than who you are at any given moment, and don't put pressure on yourself to work more than you can at any given moment. Be good to yourself. Take care of yourself. The writing will follow when it follows.

ABOUT THE AUTHOR

TIM WAGGONER has published over fifty novels and seven collections of short stories. He writes original dark fantasy and horror, as well as media tie-ins, and his articles on writing have appeared in numerous publications. He's a three-time winner of the Bram Stoker Award, has won the HWA's Mentor of the Year Award, and been a finalist for the Shirley Jackson Award, the Scribe Award, and the Splatterpunk Award. He's also a full-time tenured professor who teaches creative writing and composition at Sinclair College in Dayton, Ohio.

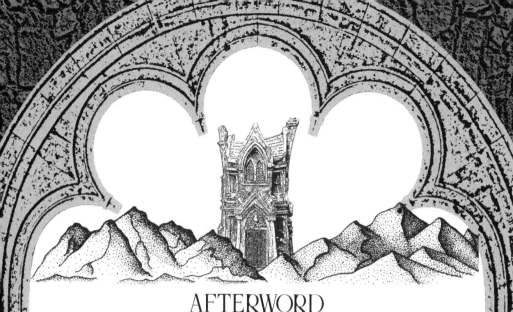

AFTERWORD

A Letter from the Vice President

My name is Meghan Arcuri, and I overuse the word *thrilled*. Sure, we all have words like this, but for this piece I wanted to challenge myself and see if I could do better. Thesaurus.com to the rescue! When I typed in *thrilled*, its only two suggestions were *elated* (yes, good one) and *atingle* (um...no, thanks). Then I tried *ecstatic*.

Bingo.

Among the thirty-seven suggestions were *crazy* and *delirious* (close), *pleased as punch* and *tickled pink* (maybe a little too cutsie?), *overjoyed* and *athrill* (better), and, once again, *elated*.

So let me just say I'm elated that StokerCon® is, once again, an in-person event. I am thrilled, overjoyed, and, yes, even pleased as punch that many of us are actually celebrating in the same room. Thank you for coming. And for those who have joined virtually: thank you for attending, as well.

As I settle into my second term as the HWA's Vice President, one thing that strikes me is how much we've grown over the past few years. At the beginning of my term in the summer of 2019, we had 1,307 members. As I write this in October 2021, we have over 1,900. And we're quickly closing in on 2,000.

For the math geeks in the room (like me), that's about a 45 percent increase in membership in just over two years.

Any number of things could contribute to this, but if I had to pick one, it would be our volunteers.

About the same time I started as VP, we needed a new volunteer coordinator. I emailed the other officers, including our awesome president, John Palisano, and kick-ass secretary, Becky Spratford, and we decided to write up a job description and email the membership.

By the end of the day, we had over a dozen people looking to fill the role.

It was an embarrassment of riches and heartening to see. But I shouldn't have been surprised. As I've said many times before, horror writers are some of the most kind and generous people I know.

All that was left was to choose someone.

In case you don't know, we chose Lila Denning. She is, in a word, amazing. A horror lover and librarian by trade, she brings organization and professionalism to the role. She has a sense of what we need and is always able to offer focus and clarity. As Becky Spratford said when she recommended Lila, if you want something done right, give it to a librarian.

With Lila and the volunteers, we have rounded out the Chapter Program Manager and Social Media teams. We've gotten assistants for the Mentorship Program and the Membership team. We've found a volunteer to put together and send iMailers to members. And we've even had a fantastic high school intern, who has been working with the Poetry Blog.

These are not the only groups in the HWA that have dedicated volunteers, of course. I could try to list all of them, but I am bound to forget someone or something. But by tightening the focus with these particular groups, by giving them more structure, more leadership, and more purpose, we have been able to increase our outreach and, thus, expand the membership of the HWA.

Across the board, our volunteers are passionate and productive, hardworking and innovative. They are problem solvers and creative thinkers. I know. I've seen it firsthand. They love horror, and their work is infused by that love, that passion for the genre.

On behalf of the officers and the Board of Trustees, I would like to thank all our volunteers for everything they to do make the HWA better. We are lucky to have you.

If you're interested in volunteering, please contact us at volunteers@ horror.org.

MEGHAN ARCURI
Vice President
Horror Writers Association

ABOUT THE HORROR WRITERS ASSOCIATION

The Horror Writers Association (HWA) is a nonprofit organization of writers and publishing professionals around the world, dedicated to promoting dark literature and the interests of those who write it. The HWA was formed in the late 1980s with the help of many of the field's greats, including Dean Koontz, Robert McCammon, and Joe Lansdale. Today, with nearly 2,000 members from across the globe, it is the oldest and most respected professional organization for the much-loved writers who have brought you the most enjoyable sleepless nights of your life.

One of the HWA's missions is to encourage public interest in and foster an appreciation of good Horror and Dark Fantasy literature. We strive to achieve this in a number of ways: we provide public areas on our website; we often sponsor or take part in public readings and lectures; we publish a blog and produce myriad materials for booksellers and librarians; we facilitate readings and signings by horror writers from our many chapters; and we sponsor StokerCon®, the premier Horror writers convention.

For more information, please visit us at https://horror.org/.

ABOUT THE BRAM STOKER AWARDS®

Each year, the Horror Writers Association presents the Bram Stoker Awards® for Superior Achievement, named in honor of Bram Stoker, author of the seminal horror work, *Dracula*. The Bram Stoker Awards® were instituted immediately after the organization's incorporation in 1987.

To ameliorate the competitive nature of any award system, the Bram Stoker Awards® are given "for superior achievement," not for "best of the year," and the rules are deliberately designed to make ties possible. The first awards were presented in 1988 (for works published in 1987) and they have been presented every year since. The award itself is an eight-inch replica of a fanciful haunted house, designed specifically for HWA by sculptor Steven Kirk. The door of the house opens to reveal a brass plaque engraved with the name of the winning work and its author.

Any work of Horror first published in the English language may be considered for an award during the year of its publication. The categories for which a Bram Stoker Award may be presented have varied over the years, reflecting the state of the publishing industry and the horror genre.

The thirteen Bram Stoker Award categories are: Novel, First Novel, Short Fiction, Long Fiction, Young Adult, Fiction Collection, Poetry Collection, Anthology, Screenplay, Graphic Novel, Nonfiction, Short Nonfiction, and Middle Grade (beginning next year).

There are two paths to a work becoming a Nominee for the Bram Stoker

Award. In one, the HWA membership at large recommends worthy works for consideration. A preliminary ballot for each category is compiled using a formula based on these recommendations. In the second, a Jury for each category also compiles a preliminary ballot. Two rounds of voting by our Active members then determine first the Final Ballot (all those appearing on the Final Ballot are "Bram Stoker Nominees"), and then the Bram Stoker Award Winners. The Winners are announced and the Bram Stoker Awards® are presented at a gala banquet, normally during the period between March and June.

ABOUT THE EDITOR

Cynthia "Cina" Pelayo is an International Latino Book Award winning and two-time Bram Stoker Awards® nominated poet and author.

She is the author of *Loteria*, *Santa Muerte*, *The Missing*, and *Poems of My Night*, all of which have been nominated for International Latino Book Awards. *Poems Of My Night* was also nominated for an Elgin Award. Her recent collection of poetry, *Into the Forest and All the Way Through* explores true crime, that of the epidemic of missing and murdered women in the United States and was nominated for a Bram Stoker Award and Elgin Award.

Her modern-day horror retelling of the Pied Piper fairy tale, *Children of Chicago* was released by Agora / Polis Books and won an International Latino Book Award for Best Mystery (2021).

Cina was raised in inner city Chicago, where she lives with her husband and children.

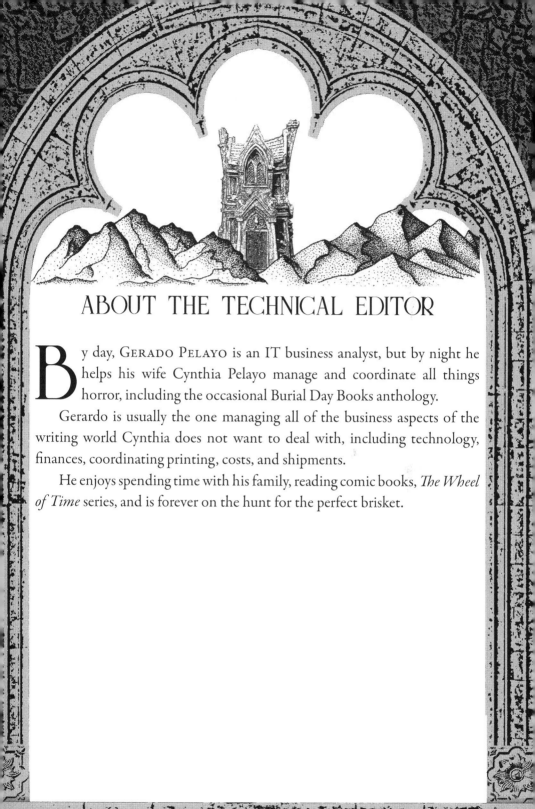

ABOUT THE TECHNICAL EDITOR

By day, GERADO PELAYO is an IT business analyst, but by night he helps his wife Cynthia Pelayo manage and coordinate all things horror, including the occasional Burial Day Books anthology.

Gerardo is usually the one managing all of the business aspects of the writing world Cynthia does not want to deal with, including technology, finances, coordinating printing, costs, and shipments.

He enjoys spending time with his family, reading comic books, *The Wheel of Time* series, and is forever on the hunt for the perfect brisket.

ABOUT THE COPYEDITOR

KARMEN WELLS is a freelance fiction editor through Shelf-Made Creative Services, specializing in substantive/developmental edits for novels and screenplays but also offering assessments and copyediting. Previously an editor in the Canadian publishing scene, most recently at HarperCollins Canada where she provided notes for authors, such as Steven Hall, Jeffrey Colvin, Jessica Westhead, and Dan Vyleta, Karmen left the corporate world to pursue working with horror writers and screenwriters and has slowly infiltrated the talented indie horror community, editing for the authors of Off Limits Press, Burial Day Books, and many self-published and spec writers. She has been a member of the HWA since 2019. And in 2021, she joined The Rights Factory as the film/TV agent where she represents screen rights for published books and has been building a horror list that includes Hailey Piper, R.J. Joseph, Daniel Barnett, Meg Hafdahl & Kelly Florence, Tim Meyer, Mike Thorn, and Jessica Guess. Karmen lives nowhere in particular and works while she travels. You can find her at www.shelfmadecreative.com or on Twitter @KarmenEdits.

ABOUT THE COVER ARTIST

Hailed by *Booklist* as "one of the most clever and original talents in contemporary horror," KEALAN PATRICK BURKE was born and raised in Ireland and emigrated to the United States a few weeks before 9/11. Since then, he has written five novels, among them the popular southern gothic slasher *Kin*, and over two hundred short stories and novellas, including *Peekers*, *Blanky*, *Sour Candy*, and *The House on Abigail Lane*, all of which are currently in development for film and TV.

A five-time Bram Stoker Award-nominee, Burke won the award in 2005 for his coming-of-age novella *The Turtle Boy*, the first book in the acclaimed Timmy Quinn series.

Most recently, he completed a new novel, *Mr. Stitch,* a collection of novellas entitled *Guests* for Suntup Editions*,* and adapted *Sour Candy* as a graphic novel for John Carpenter's Night Terrors.

Kealan is represented by Merrilee Heifetz at Writers House and Kassie Evashevski at Anonymous Content.

He lives in an unhaunted house in Ohio with a Scooby Doo lookalike rescue named Red. Follow him on Twitter @kealanburke

ABOUT THE BOOK DESIGNER

TODD KEISLING is a writer and designer of the horrific and strange. His books include *Scanlines, The Final Reconciliation, The Monochrome Trilogy,* and *Devil's Creek,* a 2020 Bram Stoker Award finalist for Superior Achievement in a Novel. A pair of his earlier works were recipients of the University of Kentucky's Oswald Research & Creativity Prize for Creative Writing (2002 and 2005), and his second novel, *The Liminal Man,* was an Indie Book Award finalist in Horror & Suspense (2013).

He works as a freelance graphic designer under the moniker of Dullington Design Co. In 2021, he was the recipient of This Is Horror's Award for Cover Art of the Year for his cover design of *Arterial Bloom,* edited by Mercedes M. Yardley and published by Crystal Lake Publishing.

Todd is an active member of the Horror Writers Association, and is represented by Italia Gandolfo, of Gandolfo Helin & Fountain Literary Management. A former Kentucky resident, he now lives somewhere in the wilds of Pennsylvania with his wife, son, and quartet of unruly cats.

SHARE HIS DREAD ONLINE
Twitter: @todd_keisling
Instagram: @toddkeisling
Patreon.com/toddkeisling
www.toddkeisling.com

ABOUT THE ILLUSTRATORS

RYAN MILLS is an illustrator and former painting instructor who has contributed work to five indie horror novels, including *Burn the Plans* by Tyler Jones (2022 Cemetery Gates Media). For more work and contact, check out his website: ryanmills.art.

LENKA ŠIMEČKOVÁ is an illustrator and comics artist from Czech Republic, with a love for macabre and dreamy atmosphere, cats and green tea. She studied at Ladislav Sutnar Faculty of Design and Art in Pilsen, and now works freelance, doing comics and illustrations for books and tabletop games.

ABOUT THE BETA READER

Ross Jeffery is the Bram Stoker Award- and Splatterpunk Award-nominated author of *Tome, Juniper, Only the Stains Remain,* and *Tethered.*

Ross's fiction has appeared in various print anthologies and his short fiction and flash fiction can be found online in many fabulous journals.

Ross lives in Bristol with his wife (Anna) and his two children (Eva and Sophie).

You can follow him on Twitter here @RossJeffery_

THE BRAM STOKER AWARDS®
COMMITTEE FOR 2021

STOKER CO-CHAIR, ADMINISTRATOR
James Chambers

STOKER CO-CHAIR, JURIES COORDINATOR, AND PUBLIC LIAISON
Jessica Landry

HEAD COMPILER
Shawnna Deresch

ASSISTANT COMPILER
Patrick Freivald

HEAD VERIFIER
Valerie Williams

ASSISTANT VERIFIERS
Kimberley Godwin, Verona Jones, Matt Henshaw

Ballot Coordinator and Webmaster
Angel Leigh McCoy

Awards Coordinator
Brian W. Matthews

2021 Awards Banquet Chairs
James Chambers, Brad C. Hodson, and Brian W. Matthews

President
John Palisano

Vice President
Meghan Arcuri

ACKNOWLEDGMENTS

THANK YOU TO OUR INTERVIEWERS

Thank you very much to our members that interviewed our Guests of Honor:

LINDA D. ADDISON
CARINA BISSETT
MICHELE BRITTANY
NICHOLAS DIAK
GABINO IGLESIAS
JONATHAN LEES
SUMIKO SAULSON

THANK YOU TO OUR VOLUNTEERS

Volunteers are essential to any community, and the HWA is no exception. We would like to thank the many members who volunteer their time to make us a successful organization. Their hard work and passion for the genre are palpable, and we appreciate them each and every day.

The HWA would also like to thank the volunteers who made StokerCon® 2022 possible. We appreciate your commitment and dedication to the convention.

Maria Abrams

Sam Anderson

Carina Bissett

Michele Brittany

Micah Castle

Ryan Croke

Shawnna Deresch

Nicholas Diak

Gabrielle Faust

April Foust

Patrick Freivald

Kimberley Godwin

Carol Gyzander

Matt Henshaw

Verona Jones

Brent Michael Kelly

Jessica Landry

Michelle Lane

Jonathan Lees

Rena Mason

Chris McAuley

Shania McCain

Morgan Minjares

Jeff Oliver

Ryan Pettis

Sarah Read

Heather Romanowski

Lindy Ryan

Sumiko Saulson

Matt Sprague

Becky Spratford

Konrad Stump

Kevin J. Wetmore, Jr.

Valerie Williams

Special thank you to StokerCon® 2022 Co-Coordinators, James Chambers and Brian W. Matthews. Each has coordinated three StokerCons: one on their own and two together. Their knowledge and expertise are invaluable; their calm demeanors and professionalism, second to none. They've had a hand in every aspect of the convention, been part of every email, every decision. We appreciate all they have done to make StokerCon® 2022 a success.

Thank you to all the people who signed up to volunteer after the printing of this book, as well.

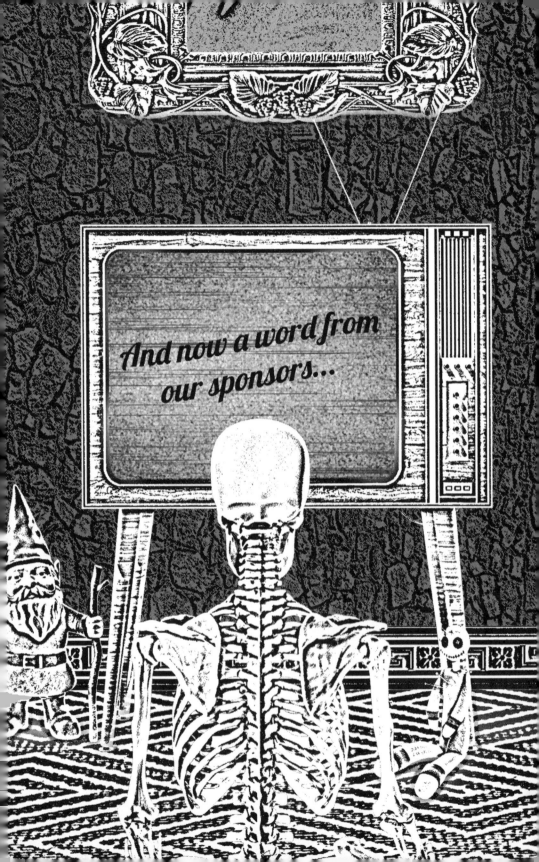

SOUVENIR BOOK SPONSORSHIPS

The Horror Writers Association is grateful to its many supporters.
We appreciate their generosity.

BEARMANOR MEDIA

BLACK & READ

BLACK SPOT BOOKS

BURIAL DAY BOOKS

DEL REY BOOKS

DRAGON'S ROOST PRESS

ERASERHEAD PRESS

GHOST ORCHID PRESS

HEX PUBLISHERS

LIBRARYREADS

MEERKAT PRESS

NOVELIST

RAW DOG SCREAMING PRESS

TOR NIGHTFIRE

ZOETIC PRESS

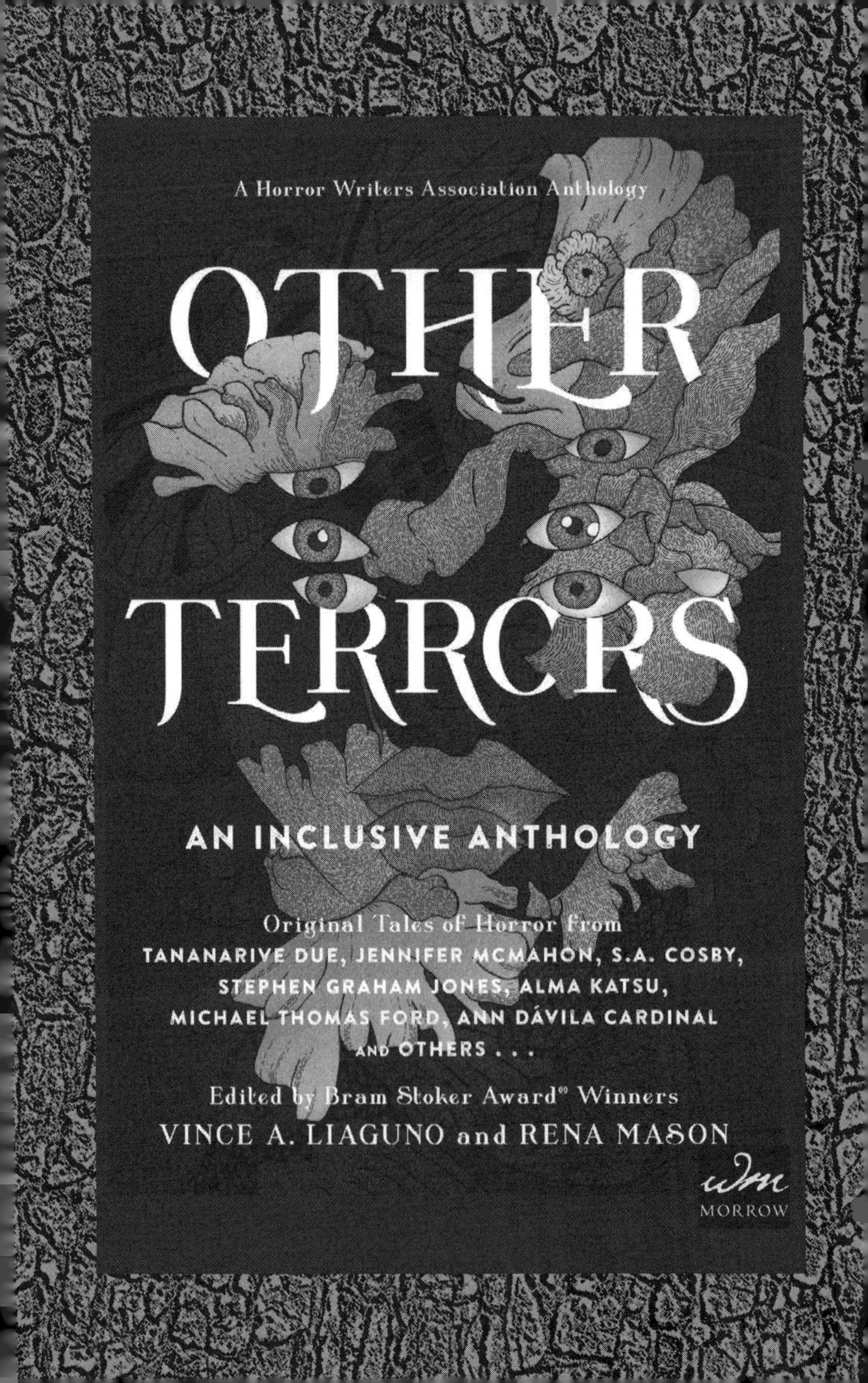
A Horror Writers Association Anthology
OTHER
TERRORS
AN INCLUSIVE ANTHOLOGY
Original Tales of Horror from
TANANARIVE DUE, JENNIFER MCMAHON, S.A. COSBY,
STEPHEN GRAHAM JONES, ALMA KATSU,
MICHAEL THOMAS FORD, ANN DÁVILA CARDINAL
AND OTHERS . . .
Edited by Bram Stoker Award® Winners
VINCE A. LIAGUNO and RENA MASON
wm
MORROW

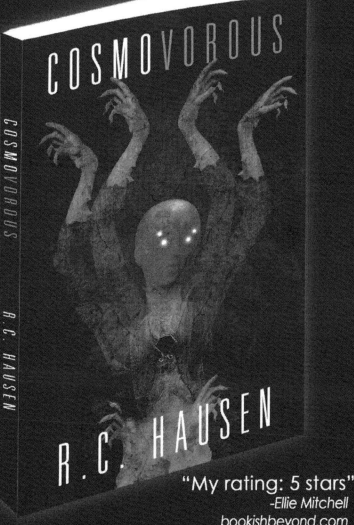

COSMOVOROUS

A COSMIC HORROR THRILLER BY

R.C. HAUSEN

"My rating: 5 stars"
-Ellie Mitchell
bookishbeyond.com

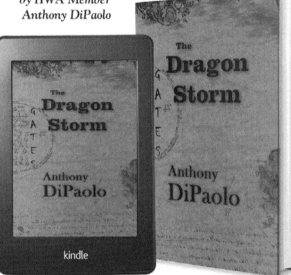

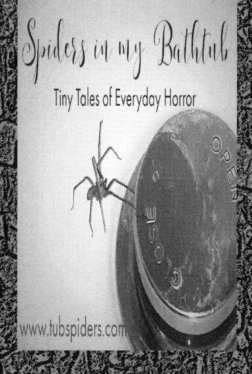

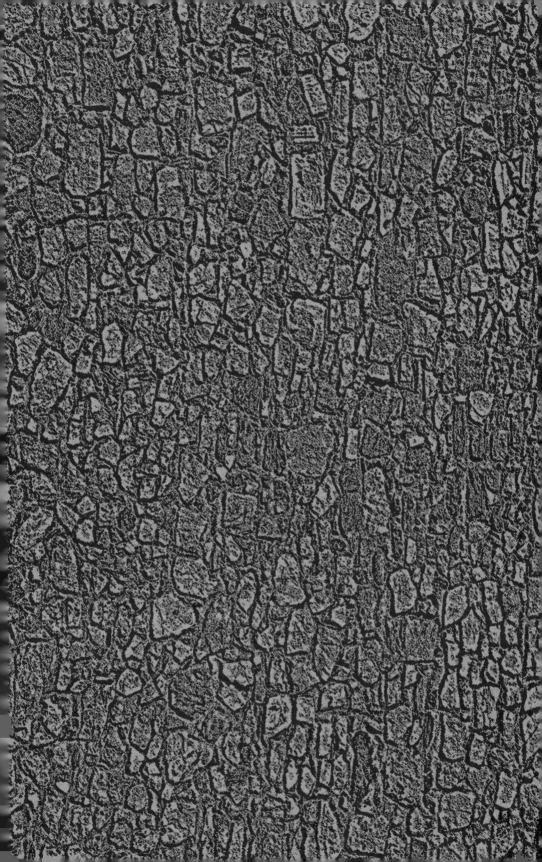

Made in the USA
Columbia, SC
22 April 2022

59331367R00183